Marwood Tucker

Michael Tresidder

A Cornish Tale: Vol. I.

Marwood Tucker

Michael Tresidder
A Cornish Tale: Vol. I.

ISBN/EAN: 9783337136949

Printed in Europe, USA, Canada, Australia, Japan

Cover: Foto ©Andreas Hilbeck / pixelio.de

More available books at **www.hansebooks.com**

MICHAEL TRESIDDER.

VOL. I.

A CORNISH TALE.

IN TWO VOLUMES.

VOL. I.

LONDON:

R. BENTLEY & SON, NEW BURLINGTON STREET.

1872.

MICHAEL TRESIDDER.

CHAPTER I.

PROLOGUE.

CHRISTMAS EVE, 1839, was a dismal night, with fierce gusts of rain and wind swirling up from seaward, and whistling through the narrow ravines, which pierced an otherwise precipitous coast. Several of these valleys starting from various points among the rocks lost themselves about two miles inland in the same thick wood, or rather forest, of old oak trees, which filled a large basin among the bleak hills, and in some places stretched up the sides, and over the rim on to the bare moorland beyond.

Down at the bottom the timber was large and handsome, but higher up it had caught the force of the sea-wind, and was twisted and stunted into many a strange form. In the middle of the hollow was a knoll, or hump of land, covered with the same half-wild forest, and with but a few spaces of clear turf here and there.

On its summit, however, stood a mass of building of fair size, and with walls of dark grey granite, almost as rugged in appearance as the mountain tors from which its stones had been originally hewn. One side of this, with three projecting gables, that in the centre having a deep porch under it, faced seawards down the wildest and most picturesque of the wooded glens; and by the occasional glimpses of moonlight when the black clouds happened to be blown asunder for a short minute or two, a saddled horse might be seen standing upon the gravel terrace in front, with his bridle hung over an old-fashioned hook placed for that purpose near the door. The poor animal every now and then shook himself roughly, when the storm came down with more than usual vehemence, but was prevented by the shortness of the rein from obtaining any shelter in the broad and deeply-recessed archway of the porch.

Streaks of coloured light shone through two wide mullioned windows of old stained glass, and often formed themselves into mimic rainbows upon the cold wet mist outside. The promise, however, which they seemed to give of bright happiness as well as of warmth within, was unfulfilled by the reality.

They were the windows of a very large and lofty apartment, which, if the great entrance door had not opened under a gallery at one end, would have been called a sitting-room; and if the signs of constant use and occupation had not been scattered about on chair and table might certainly have been considered a mere hall. The furniture, like the panelling of the walls and screen in front of the gallery, was black with age, and rich with antique carving; but the tapestry which covered them was faded, while the chairs themselves were designed rather for state than pleasure, or even comfort. Being such as they were, they assorted well enough with the elder of the two men, who were the only occupants of the room.

The master, for it was impossible to doubt that such was his position in the house, was not much above middle age, and about middle height, but so unflinchingly upright in bearing that he appeared much taller.

He had a strong spare figure which showed to advantage in the hunting dress, which he and his companion both wore; and his left hand, as he stood before the arched fireplace, still grasped with hard bony fingers the heavy whip he had brought home two hours before. His face if there had been any touch of softness in it, would have been as handsome as it certainly was distinguished. Forehead high, nose, mouth and chin well formed and, as a matter of course thirty years ago, not hidden by any moustache or beard. The complexion, too, had the clear brown which much out door exercise usually gives, but the eyes were too near together, and disagreeable from the intense, overweening pride and obstinacy which shone through them.

His companion was, from the strong likeness between the two, evidently his son, but he was taller and slighter than his father, and although his face at that moment had much of the stern look which characterised that of the other, it was easy to see that its more general expression was soft and gentle.

"Father," he said, advancing somewhat nearer to him but still remaining
with one hand resting on the great table
that stood in the centre of the room.
"I am sorry that as we rode home
together I should have mentioned Ellen
at all. I am more sorry that since we
have been disputing here these two hours,
I should have allowed myself to say
to you many words that your son
ought not to have uttered. But my
honour as well as my love is concerned.
It is impossible that I can be false to
my word, and renouncing Ellen, marry
this lady you have chosen for me. She
may be, as you say, most beautiful; she
may be also a little the superior in birth,
but she is, I am confident, infinitely
less worthy than her in everything
else."

The young man who appeared to be about twenty-five, spoke with both pathos and dignity; but his father was equally unmoved by either. Opposition did not make him openly angry, in the manner that most men are affected by it, but caused the pupils of his blue eyes to contract and glitter like steel.

"Do not talk to me," he said sternly, "of your promise to this beggar girl with whom you have chosen to fancy yourself in love; I tell you once again that I would rather see you dead than married to her. No doubt she is, for all her simple looks, some scheming wanton, who is already boasting of her conquest of the rich young fool, and would care little enough for you without your money."

At this coarse abuse of his betrothed,

the young man was provoked beyond all endurance, and his look became equal in firmness to that of his father. Drawing himself up to his full height, he answered with much dignity—

"Sir, although you appear to do so, I cannot forget, that I am a gentleman, and I cannot stay here to listen to language which insults the lady I love, and yet which I may not resent. It is not even possibly true, for Ellen can be no schemer, since she does not know that I am rich, does not even know my real name. Wealth and family connexion appear to you everything. I will show you that I can be as proud of poverty and friendlessness, as you are of riches and position. From this night I renounce for ever the father who has insulted me, and I leave to him the absolute possession of that property which he cares for more than for his son's happiness; and of that name which he thinks will be disgraced by loyalty to a plighted word."

As he thus spoke, he turned away, and taking his hat from the table, walked towards the door. When half way, he turned once more to his father, and walking back to him, put out his hand.

" Tell me you did not mean what you said, father. You could not have intended to speak as you did."

The older man, who had been slightly shaken from his scornful composure by his son's unusual manliness, and had followed his movements across the room with a faint look of respect and even affection, now unfortunately regarded this speech as a mere sign of weakness, not as springing from the strong filial sense of love which had actually prompted it.

" Not mean what I said " he replied contemptuously, " indeed I meant it thoroughly, as I always do. I am not a boy to waste my breath in mere idle vapourings to which I have not courage to adhere."

The son stopped suddenly and stood for an instant as if stunned by this taunting reply to the words, which he had only after a great struggle brought himself to utter. Then, without any attempt to speak again, he retraced his steps across the Hall. This time he did not turn, but walking with a firm and steady tread to the door, passed through it and out of the house into the driving mist and rain.

The horse whinnied on his appearance, as if glad to see his rider, but wondering that he was not taken as usual to his warm stable. He was patted kindly, but the bridle was unhooked, and as the young man mounted, he said half to the horse, and half to himself.

"You will come back to your old shelter, Connorree, before many hours are past; but I have left mine for life."

The expression of his face was that of deep sorrow; but there was no sign of any repentance for the step he had taken.

As he rode slowly down the knoll upon which his father's house stood, and taking a road which seemed to run parallel to the coast, he quickened his pace to a gallop, and had soon plunged into the stormy darkness, which completely hid all the lower ground from view.

At the old Manor House they told the Squire on the next, the Christmas morning, that the young master's horse had been brought home by old John Hawken; and there was much talk about the place, as to the reason of his sudden departure; but no one dared to speak of it to the father.

He himself did not say a word on the subject, and was indeed at all times too proud to talk much to his servants; but his face had a restless look, and his eyes constantly turned to the door when it opened. Yet, when a week afterwards, a letter came in the son's writing, and with a London postmark, his father's anger seemed to return. He wrote at once a few short lines of answer, then crushed the note he had received under his heel, and threw it into the fire before he rode off to post his reply himself.

Many years passed away, and each Christmas as it came, found the old man's upright figure a trifle less erect. The restless expectant look became habitual to him, he ceased to hunt and even to care for his hounds and horses; and he would sit for hours together on one side of the old-fashioned fire-place with his eyes fixed upon the empty arm-chair opposite, which his son had been used to occupy.

To his household and his tenants his manner became more reserved even

than before, and acquired a certain
air of defiance; as if guessing that they
blamed him for the young man's absence, but daring them to show that
they did so. With kindly instinct they
divined his thoughts, pitied whilst they
feared him; and for his sake kept
from every incidental allusion to the
absent man.

"Poor Squire," some one or the other
of them would say in the steward's
room, or at the village club, "he's a
terrible hard man sure enough, and it
'ud take a brave bit of trouble to
make he feel: but 'tis easy to see his
heart's a grieving sore about young
master, and that he's a breaking
fast."

In this they were right, the tenth
Christmas Eve had come to the wild

hollow; and had found the Lord of the Manor a mere wreck of the stalwart figure he had been in 1839. His old butler, who had grown to know his wishes from the merest look or sign, observed that during dinner he was scarcely able to touch any food; and as soon as he was left alone, he took something from his breast, round which his hand seemed to have been almost constantly clasped the whole afternoon. It was the portrait of his boy. As he looked at this, he put his arms forward on the great table, just where his son's hand had rested during their last interview and after gazing intently upon the picture for some time, he let his head fall forward wearily upon his clasped fingers.

When the old servant entered later

in the evening to close the Hall for
the night, he went to rouse his master
from sleep, as he thought, but found
that he was gone past all wakening.
That he was dead.

CHAPTER II.

THIRTY years have passed away, and two Englishmen are contemplating one of the prettiest views of the lovely Bay of Naples, namely that from the windows of the Trattoria Scoglia di Frisio. The scene is framed by the vine-clad trellis of the balcony, and has the ruddy brown mass of the ruin, called that of Queen Joanna's

Palace, in the foreground to the left, with the scrambling pile of villas on the hill side above it, just crowned with a fringe of green towards Virgil's Tomb. Beyond this, runs the sweeping curve of the fine parade called the Riviera di Chiaja, separated from the blue waters of the Mediterranean by the Villa Reale gardens, and stretching on to the Chiata Monte point, and the Castell' dell' Ovo. Above, the picture is completed by the slope of sunburnt town as it climbs pell-mell up the hill towards St. Elmo, of which the angles and bastions stand out sharp and clear against the bright sky.

Beyond this point the line of seashore, which has been hidden in the long retiring curve of the Spiaggia

di Marinella, is again visible as it
nears Portici, and white specks of building dot the slopes of Vesuvius. That
capricious mountain looks pretty and
innocent with its bold outline, many
coloured sides and the soft wreath of
silver smoke which is crowning its
summit gracefully; while Monte St.
Angelo and the distant hills towards
Sorrento glisten every now and then
out of their purple haze, as the sun
catches them on this September afternoon.

"So you really must go home-
wards, Michael," said a dark highbred
looking man of three-and-twenty, who
was enjoying from the balcony the
scene we have attempted to describe,
and whose pale hollow cheeks, but
lively brown eyes showed that he

was recovering from a serious illness.
"Well, I am very sorry, and shall
not soon forget the care you have
taken of me all these weeks. Our
Government is much given to dis-
embarrassing the country of places
where a soldier can enjoy life; it is
to be hoped that they will in fact
apply the same principle to the bad
quarters, and make over the wretched
island of Malta to the Pope, as report
says, or to any other distressed poten-
tate, who will engage to live there
during the summer months."

"The sooner the better, Ellerton,
especially as His Holiness seldom appears dressed in anything but white
from top to toe : the rules of etiquette
are not generally so well suited to circumstances, as such a costume would be

to the streets of Valetta under a scorching August sun."

The last speaker, Michael Tresidder, has a pleasant Saxon face, softened rather than concealed by a short curly beard and moustache of bright fair hair. This is lit up by a pair of grey blue eyes, which atone for their somewhat negative colour by rapid changes of expression, their most constant look, however, being that of half-amused, wholly good-tempered criticism of what may be going on before them.

This sort of countenance is common among young Englishmen, who have found the world open before them pleasantly; but when, as in the case of Tresidder, there are indications of energy and resolution lying half-hidden under the smooth surface, it does not

argue that the owner is at all less
capable of grappling with the realities
of mature life, than he has been to
share in the active pleasures of boyhood.

Lord Ellerton, who had spoken first,
was at this time an officer in the 23rd
Welsh Fusiliers, quartered at Malta. Last
spring, Tresidder happened to come to
that picturesque, but unhealthy quarter,
on his way home after several years
wandering in the Mediterranean in a
schooner yacht of some two hundred
and fifty tons.

The two men had grown to be great
allies, and when Ellerton was attacked
during the moist clammy heat of a
Maltese summer by low fever, Tresidder
had remained to nurse him, and as
soon as he was sufficiently recovered

had brought him, on board the yacht,
away to Naples. They had now been
some three weeks cruising about the
bay, or landing to make short excur-
sions on shore. Few illnesses pass off
more slowly than does this fever, and
although the friends had walked but a
short way this afternoon, Lord Ellerton
was greatly fatigued, and was lying
propped up by cushions on two of those
spindle-legged broad-seated chairs, with
an occasional patch of tarnished gilding
to recall their former magnificence,
which are to be found in every Italian
house, however humble.

The furniture of this and of most
similar hostelries has certainly gone down
in the world, and probably once adorned
some palace like that of which the ruins
are just below. So also the timbers

of the balcony, on which the friends are sitting, have no doubt been filched from their once lordly neighbour; but the retribution was sufficiently just, for of that in turn the marble and carved stone work were certainly stolen from some building of the Imperial age.

A bright Algerian wrapper, which his invalid state of health still rendered necessary, concealed Lord Ellerton's figure, but he is evidently tall, and his broad shoulders, and the long masculine fingers of one hand which rests upon the arm of the chair, showed that he was before this attack of Maltese fever both well grown and powerful.

Michael Tresidder is of middle stature only, but his slight well-knit frame and active bearing prevent this want of height from being noticeable. He is sittiug on the rail of the balcony, and with one hand shading his eyes, watches through an opera glass the movements of the sailors on board a small schooner unmistakeably an English yacht, which is at anchor in the Spiaggia di Chiaja, that is to say, in the bay between them and the Castell' dell' Ovo.

"I told Harris to get the 'Ariel,' ready, George, so as to start very early to-morrow morning should you wish it, and am glad to see they are all busy on board. It would be rather slow work for you to remain on here alone; and if you slip quietly round the coast to Messina, and wait about there a bit till the weather becomes cooler, you can reach 'Nix Manjare' comfortably, by the time your leave is up."

"Thank you," said Lord Ellerton, "that will do famously for me, but it is a great shame to let another man sail about luxuriously in your 'Ariel,' while you pitchfork yourself into a greasy coasting-steamer among a crowd of gesticulating Italians. They are brown enough by nature, goodness knows, without any additional necessity for ignoring as they do the existence of soap and water."

"Never mind the natives," laughed Tresidder. "I like them, and upon my honour, I believe they like me. I think I have told you that I was last at Naples in 1860, just as Garibaldi made that stroke, unexampled in history, and took a kingdom captive at

the point of his umbrella, or some such
deadly weapon. They say Ferdinand
thought that the quiet carriage and
pair, in which the General and his staff
of three companions entered from the
railway station, was filled with some
powerful explosive of a new description, and so it was; but of a moral
not material species. The powder was
strong enough to upset king, queen,
courtiers, and army in a twinkling,
and all Naples turned itself out of
window to welcome the popular dic-
tator. Talk of gesticulating Italians,
you should have seen the Toledo then!
Such a scene I certainly never witnessed;
all the carpets had become balcony-
hangings, and all the curtains banners
across the street; while the chatter
of the most talkative population in

Europe was aggravated to a frantic pitch."

" Well, the town is pretty enough for me even without them," said Lord Ellerton, " what charming pictures Margaret would have made had she been here. Remember, Michael, you have promised to pay my people a visit as soon as you get home; I think you will like them, and Healey is a pretty place. They can give you a fair day's sport too."

"Oh, I am quite ready to go, I assure you," replied Michael laughing, "and as I am anxious to earn your fair cousin and *fiancée's* favour, I am glad to be able to report that you will soon be quite strong. Lady Margaret must be quite beautiful from your description."

"She is very beautiful," said Ellerton, "but we have known each other so long, and grown up together so much like brother and sister, that we do not, either of us, I think, go in for much of the rhapsody of young love."

"She was anxious enough when you were ill," put in the other.

"Oh, yes; I suppose Margaret would have been shocked at my death, but I doubt if her sorrow for me would have been half as great as that of my mother. However, as I am not dead yet," Lord Ellerton added, laughing, "I do not know that the question is worth considering, especially as we are to be married early in next year if I get out of the regiment by that time. I hope we shall meet in England by February,

Michael, for you know you are to be my best man."

"All right, George, I shall be ready; but you certainly will not be at a wedding in three months' time, if you stay out in this balcony till the evening damp comes on; remember you are to treat yourself quite as an invalid for some while yet."

"You are a kind nurse, Michael," said his friend, looking at him affectionately as he prepared to move.

"All selfishness," laughed Tresidder, "think what a pleasant reception I should get at Healey, if instead of good news I was obliged to confess to Lady Ferndale that I had just heard from Antoine, and that your fever had returned."

Leaving that accomplished Frenchman,

who had followed his master during all
his wanderings, but was now to remain
as doctor in charge of Lord Ellerton, to
settle their bill and bring the carriage
and wrappers after them down the hill,
Tresidder rose as he spoke, and with
his friend, who as yet required support
in walking, strolled quietly towards the
town.

The Trattoria at which they had dined,
is as favourite a resort of Neapolitans
as Richmond and Greenwich are of
Londoners, and is situated upon the new
Posilippo road which skirts the shore
beyond the Mergellina, and climbs the
hill of Capo Coroglio which the grotto
of Pozzuoli avoids.

The distance is only about a mile,
but Ellerton's strength was exhausted
long before they reached the beginning

of the Chiaja, **and he was** glad **to rest**
by the roadside till the carriage over-
took them. Driving rapidly through
the crowd of vehicles of all descriptions
—from a luxurious English barouche
with its pair of spirited horses, to the
humble Neapolitan calessino rattling behind a queer little steed of more courage
than beauty — which always throngs
the Chiaja at this period of the afternoon, the two friends soon reached
the landing place at Sta. Lucia, where
the gig of the "Ariel" was waiting to
carry them on board.

The trim English sailors, with their
clean white trousers, and white shirts
edged with blue, with "Ariel" worked
.upon the breast, were exchanging jokes
with the numerous half-clad, olive-
-skinned Lazzaroni, who are at all times

to be found lounging about the steps, eating maccaroni, or haggling for cheap fish.

Neither party understood a word of the others' language, but the Italians rattled away with much gesture and a good display of white teeth, while the yachtsmen replied by benevolent smiles and grunts of patronising good-nature, such as only English sailors can achieve.

The steamer for Civita Vecchia, by which Tresidder had to travel, was already getting up her steam, and there was only time to have Lord Ellerton comfortably settled on board the schooner before it was necessary for his friend to follow his luggage, which had been already sent to the larger vessel.

" Good-bye, George, I hope they will

take good care of you. Remember me to
the old 23rd when you get to Malta. We
shall meet in a few months in England,
and both of us, I suppose, have to begin
life in earnest. Good-bye, Captain Harris;
mind you don't wreck his Lordship on
Scylla or in Charybdis."

One more hearty shake of Ellerton's
hand, and Michael Tresidder jumped again
into his gig, and managed to reach the
steamer and clamber up her sides as the
paddles began to move.

While the "Popolo Romano" steamed
out of the bay, he stood leaning over the
bulwarks and watched the graceful little
vessel, which had been his home for so
many months, until she was hidden by
Capo Coroglio, as the steamer rounded
that point and crossed the harbour of
Pozzuoli. All the time he was able to

distinguish Lord Ellerton, in an invalid
chair near the stern of the "Ariel," and
frequently waved his hand to his friend;
but Tresidder's last glimpse of his yacht
was brightened by the sight of her sailors
springing into the shrouds to wave their
red caps, and give him a parting
cheer.

At the same moment the white ensign
of the Squadron, flying at her peak, was
dipped in salute, and a puff of smoke from
her bows, followed by a slight report,
showed her master that the "Ariel" was
unwilling to let him leave her without due
honour.

The "Popolo Romano," until she had
cleared Capo Miseno, and for a few
minutes while passing between the island
of Procida and the mainland, hovered on
the edge of the two bays of Gaëta and

of Naples, had been steering into the eye
of the setting sun ; and Michael, looking
back over the taffrail, had the entire
circuit of the beautiful gulf before him,
from Pozzuoli and Miseno on the north,
to Sorrento and the island of Capri
on the south.

All at this hour of the evening,
and in this month of September, were
bathed in a wonderfully brilliant haze
of ruddy gold and of faint ethereal
purple.

Fashion has taught men to believe
that the climate of every place south
of Florence is unendurable up to a
late period of the autumn, or the beginning of winter ; but those who follow
her dictates have little opportunity of
learning what is the real force and
beauty of the tints that can be mixed

on nature's palette. The canvas on which she paints here, in Southern Italy, will not, it is true, bear close inspection; for the entire soil of the country round Naples has, by the blazing heat of June, July, and August, been caked over with a hard seamy crust, suggestive only of some one or other of the circles of Dante's Inferno; but the colours out of which the picture is blended, would seem to have been invented and ground in Paradise.

CHAPTER III.

BY merely a slight effort, the entire attention frees itself from all immediate surroundings, so soon as the resolution to enter upon a different course of action has been taken; and all one's thoughts become rapidly absorbed in plans for the future, or in recollections of the distant past, of which the half-forgotten influences are again coming into play.

In his rapid journey to Paris, Michael
Tresidder paid flying visits to Rome,
Pisa, and Genoa, but carried away from
all three little but the memory of one
moonlight ramble round the Forum and
Coliseum, and one exquisite sunset on
the Carrara Mountains, as he traversed
the beach at La Spezzia. He had
started on his voyage nearly five years
since, full of romantic ardour for the
beautiful and picturesque, and with
every appliance for painting that the
ingenuity of all the art-colourmen in
London could supply. But the constant
companionship of his fine vigorous crew
of west country sailors, coupled with
the variety of people of all nations and
all ranks with whom at every port he
had associated, had taught Tresidder to
regard the actors, and even the super-

numeraries, on the world's stage, as
of more interest than the most completely charming display of scenery.

His father had been the head of an
old Cornish family, almost equal, as
many of such families are, in point of
antiquity to the rugged hills or widely
sweeping moors amongst which they
have lived; but owners at no period
during all these years of more than a
few thousand acres of wild ground,
half cultivation, half common; one or
two romantic glades of trees and of old
coppice, very suggestive of woodcocks
to the eye of a sportsman; and two
or three miles of grand cliff scenery,
bounding a sea of such brilliant green,
as only the north coast of Cornwall
can produce.

Colonel Tresidder, of Portruan Manor,

spent his youth in the army, and had
reached middle age before he succeeded
a distant cousin in the property; and,
when quartered at an Irish town, fell
desperately in love with, and, after a
short but energetic courtship, married
Lord Kilfenora's lovely daughter of nine-
teen—Lady Eveline Fitzgerald.

Soon afterwards he settled down at
home, and was persuaded not only to
grant setts (as leases for mining purposes are called) on two or three of
his barren fields, where indications of
copper had been observed, but also to
become a considerable sharer in the
undertaking of his lessees.

Unlike many of these underground
speculators, the Adventurers of Wheal
Eveline and Wheal Tresidder met with
enormous success, and within ten years

of his marriage and settlement in the old house of Portruan, Colonel Tresidder had realised a considerable fortune, and yet was still in receipt of a very large addition to his territorial income from the mining dues.

Soon after this he died, leaving his only son Michael to the guardianship of Lady Eveline, who, like so many really high-bred Irish women, was possessed of sound common sense, high feeling, and even considerable talent, no less than she was distinguished by a merry, spirited, and chivalrous disposition, and a generous sympathy for the failings, as well as the sorrows, of her neighbours, poor as well as rich.

Their home, as the Colonel became wealthy, had been with great taste and care extended and improved, till the old granite Manor-house, which though always stately and picturesque was not originally extensive, had developed into one of the most spacious, and quite the most attractive looking country house in the West of England.

Lady Eveline, who detested an effeminate boy as much as her country-women generally do, encouraged Michael's natural taste for riding and other outdoor amusements heartily; shared in his pleasures, if possible, and when her widowhood and more mature age made her own appearance in the hunting-field no longer desirable, always talked over the day's run with the youngster, and took care to keep up her close acquaintance with the country-side, so as to understand the more thoroughly his description.

The result of such a community of

interest was, that Michael united not a little of the youth's fondness for a merry and pleasant companion, to the loving veneration he felt for his beautiful mother.

While at Eton and Oxford, he was perpetually bringing to Portruan, during the holidays and vacations, some of his numerous school and college friends. They were always heartily welcomed, and treated by Lady Eveline with warm courtesy, mixed with a little of that ceremonious regard which, if not carried too far, is especially captivating to a boy or very young man from a handsome woman.

Young Tresidder could, however, seldom be persuaded to visit his friends in return.

" No, no, mother," he would say, in

answer to her pressing request for him to go to this or that pleasant house. " Let them come here by all means, and as many as you please. I like the Trebartha girls very much, and Jack Martineau and his minor are capital fellows; but I have only just come back to my lady-love, and am not going to let her send me off again yet."

The years ran on in this pleasant though uneventful fashion, marked only by a few short trips together to the Continent, till after Michael had come of age, and had taken his degree with some little distinction at Oxford.

He had become the actual possessor of Portruan, and, in addition to eight or ten thousand a year, which was the present value of the settled pro-

perty, his trustees had made over to
him the large sum to which the ready
money left by his father, and the accu-
mulations during his own long minority
amounted.

His mother now urged him strongly
to travel for a few years, and persuaded him to go up to Cowes during
the Regatta week, and stay, as he
had been often asked to do, with
Ronald Farquharson, who was Com-
modore of the Royal Yacht Squadron,
and whose fag he had been at Eton.

The result of his visit was the pur-
chase of the "Ariel." Leaving her to
be thoroughly refitted and stocked for
a long voyage, Michael came back to
Portruan to collect a crew from among
the bronzed fishermen of the hamlet,
within a mile of his house, whose

comrade in many a day and night of hardy sport he had already often been.

Preparations, where money is plenty, do not take very long, and within six weeks the beautiful schooner, exquisitely fitted and equipped from her keel to the trucks of her dainty rakish masts, glided under Pendennis Castle and dropped her anchor in Falmouth Harbour, to wait the arrival of her new owner.

The following day Michael and Lady Eveline drove across from the north coast to inspect her, and within a week mother and son had parted for their first long separation.

Since then, numerous letters had passed between them, but absence and change of scene rapidly teach a man

to rely upon himself and his own re-
sources.

Michael's affection for Lady Eveline
was not less, but it had changed in
character with his own progress in men-
tal activity. There was perhaps greater
strength of feeling, but there was certainly less of dependence in it. All
this the mother had foreseen. She acknowledged to herself that, with all his
manliness and muscular energy, her son
would never fully develope into the
sort of man she considered him capable
of becoming, until he was thrown entirely, and for some lengthened period,
upon his own guidance, and was forced
to form his own unaided opinion as to
men and things. She noticed with
pleasure, and without any of the pain
which a sentimental person might have

experienced, the slight increase of self-assertion in the tone of his letters, and the hasty warmth of some of his conclusions.

Good judgment, like a good seat across country, only in a very small degree comes by nature, and is principally due to the number and variety of a man's intellectual sommersaults. The rider who has not the courage to risk a fall will never lead the field. The scholar, the statesman, even the talker, who has not nerve enough to hazard a bold conjecture, or enter on a resolute line of action, if there is any chance of its turning out a failure, will never make much of a mark in the world.

Tresidder had been absent from England about a year, when Lady Eveline,

who had long known herself to be
in delicate health, though she had
concealed the fact from her son,
died after only a few days' serious
illness.

Knowing when the last attack began,
that its fatal result could not be delayed long enough for Michael to return
from the coast of Norway, where he
then was, in time to see her alive, she
would allow no message to be sent to
call him home.

On the contrary, she desired that the
few lines of farewell, which she managed
to write at intervals, as her weakness
would permit, should not be forwarded
until after her death. In them, she
affectionately excused her conduct in
hiding her illness from him, and begged
that his wanderings might be continued

at least as long as had been originally intended.

The shock experienced by the young man when he received the letter from his uncle, Lord Kilfenora, which announced the death of that mother, whom he had almost idolised, was naturally great.

His first impulse had been to rebel against her last wishes, and hasten back at once to the scenes which would remind him of their happy life together. As he felt, however, the assistance which the clear cold Norwegian atmosphere and wild scenery of the Fjords gave to him in subduing the first violence of grief, he acknowledged that she was right, as usual, in her judgment of what would be most likely to promote his happiness; and, after a time, he grew to dread, rather than wish, to hasten the time for returning home.

When his Northern cruise was completed, he had come southwards to the Mediterranean, without any inclination to visit England on the way, and had regained his old light-hearted spirit among the islands of the Ægean, and the exquisite scenery of the Golden Horn and the coast of Asia Minor.

In one of his many ramblings on shore, he had seen more than most Englishmen of beautiful but semi-barbarous Greece, whose political condition at the present day is more anarchical than that of Mexico, while the domestic security and morality of its inhabitants are scarcely greater than those of an African tribe.

At another time he had penetrated
the grand defiles of the Caucasus, and
striking from Georgia southwards, reached
Palestine and Jerusalem by a route as
interesting as it is difficult, and rarely·
attempted.

Now, as the distance between him
and England rapidly diminished, the
traveller found his thoughts grouping
themselves more and more closely round
home affairs, and speculations as to what
should· be his future course.

He knew that he would probably be
expected to take part in local politics;
and that if any vacancy should occur
in the representation of the county,
most of his neighbours would look to
him to come forward and contest the
seat.   But he was amused by considering how far some of the political

notions which he had begun to entertain would agree with their old-fashioned
Toryism.

Just then he reached the termi-
nus in the Boulevard Mazas, in the
grey of an autumn morning, after the
long run from Lyons, and had to assist
the young Cornish man (who had come
with him from the yacht in Antoine's place,
but to whom French was an unknown
tongue) to collect his various belongings.
As he drove across Paris, boiling as
it then was with the excitement of
the revolution which followed the battle
of Sedan, he pictured to himself the
horror with which Squire Trecarrels,
of Trecarrels, who had proposed every
Tory candidate in Cornwall for the last
fifty years, would hear him confess the
belief that manhood suffrage, whether

desirable or not in England, was after all merely the practical acknowledgment of that right of the people to influence the exercise of power upon which, theoretically, our constitution had always insisted.

CHAPTER IV

EAR MR. TRESIDDER,

" We hear from Ellerton that a letter will find you at the Traveller's on your way through town, and I hope to persuade you to delay your return home for a few days, and allow Lord Ferndale and myself to have the pleasure of making your acquaintance and thanking you for your great kindness to George.

" We have not a very large party

at Healey at present, but there are two
or three people whom you know, or
know about; and your cousin, Bertie
Cunninghame, who is here, begs me
to say that he has three very important reasons for wishing you to
come.

" These are; that he and my third
son Robert are just now the only
sportsmen, and it is impossible with but
two guns to do justice to a single
covert next Saturday; that you are the
only man of his acquaintance sufficiently Saxon in appearance to make
a series of tableaux, which he is bent
on producing next week, successful; and
lastly, that he has some weighty political matters upon which he must talk
to you.

" There is a very nice Great Northern

train from London, which reaches Matfield, our station, at half-past five in
the afternoon, and we will send there
to meet you on Thursday, or any
other day that you will tell me we
may have the pleasure of expecting
you.

 " Believe me,

  " Dear Mr. Tressider,

   " Sincerely yours,

    " ELIZABETH FERNDALE.

" Healey Towers,

" Monday, September 26th."

An envelope directed to him in a
bold feminine hand, and stamped with
a silver and black monogram of the
letters E. F., under a Countess' coronet,
had been given to him by the porter at
the " Traveller's;" as, soon after his

arrival in London, Tresidder strolled down from his hotel in Dover Street to dine at that comfortable and highly respectable club.

On opening it, he had found this cordial invitation from the mother of his friend Lord Ellerton, to pay a visit at the Yorkshire house, about which he had heard much during their evening talks on board the " Ariel."

As there was no real necessity for his immediate return to Cornwall, he wrote at once a few lines of pleased acceptance to Lady Ferndale, but delayed his arrival until the Friday, as, after such long absence from conventional life, his tailor would require a day or two to fit him out properly. He was not more of a dandy than most other young men of his class, but knew, from the fact of his volatile cousin's presence at Healey, that he would find the house occupied by what that young gentleman called the right sort of people.

Bertie Cunninghame possessed every material qualification for a life of fashionable pleasure, except the useful item of money ; and every requisite talent for the achievement of really considerable success in serious business, except the invaluable power of steadily adhering, for any length of time, to the pursuit of one object.

Well born and well connected — his father was a Warwickshire squire, and his mother a sister of Lady Eveline Tresidder—his good looks and power of keeping people amused, without fatiguing them, or even allowing them to suppose that they did not not amuse themselves, made him an agreeable unit of society in town, but an invaluable acquisition to the party at a country house.

When a man has a choice, he usually chooses the best; and although Bertie was too well-bred ever to let any reason but that of accident appear for his acceptance of one rather than another of his numerous invitations for the Autumn, you were pretty sure to find that the party which had been most successful, and left the largest quantity of pleasant memories up to the following Spring, had alone included him among the guests.

As a rule, it is difficult to say, whether to a man who is unfortunately in town at the end of September, it is preferable that the wholesome process of scrubbing and carpet-beating should go on at his own club, or at his neighbour's.

It is actively unpleasant to be turned out of a pet corner, and forced to explain your peculiar views as to chili vinegar or white pepper to strange waiters; but it is passively disagreeable, especially if you are a somewhat crusty old bachelor, to see strange faces of " fellows whom nobody knows, you know," and for whom you, of course, feel a proper contempt, usurping the chairs in the library, or the couches in the smoking-room, which are associated with your own absent friends. To a mere bird of passage, however, like Tresidder, the pursuit of cleanliness which had thrown the " Athenæum " on the hospitality of the " Traveller's," was welcome rather than not, as it gave him a better chance of meeting any acquaintance who might chance to be detained in London, or be a casual wayfarer like himself.

While ordering his own dinner, he was warmly accosted by a rather short and thick-set man of between forty and fifty years of age, the lower part of whose face was entirely disguised by a thick black beard, but whose well-cut aquiline nose, and deeply sunk dark eyes under strongly-marked eyebrows, were surmounted by a forehead much furrowed by lines of care and thought, but of astonishing breadth and height.

Giuseppe Mola was by birth a Piedmontese, but had been sent in boyhood as a scholar to the Royal Seminary at

Naples. He was, however, expelled from thence on account of some witty sarcasms upon Ferdinand, and during all the years of his opening manhood, from seventeen to twenty-three, had been an inmate of various State prisons.

At first, he had been kept under close restraint, but not deprived of books and other materials for study ; afterwards, either from some opinions which he had incautiously stated in conversation with a fellow-prisoner, and which might have been overheard, or from a mere freak of despotism, he had been sent to Ishia, and made to occupy, with a number of other unfortunates, some political offenders but others criminals of the ordinary and degraded class, one of the lowest and most repulsive of the dungeons in the castle on the rock Negrone.

His youth, however, gave him courage to attempt and succeed in making an escape that seemed well nigh impossible; and his whole life since that time had been devoted to the furtherance, with more or less success, of various schemes for promoting Italian liberty and unity.

Tresidder and Mola had become acquainted at Naples in 1860, and the Italian's energetic and enthusiastic character had combined—with the interest naturally attaching to a man who had risked his life over and over again for a great cause, and spent in confinement, and even in chains, the years that to most of us fly pleasantly past at school and college—to make a permanent impression upon the young Englishman.

"Well met, Signor Tresidder. I am glad to see you again, and have often feared that I had cut your mind adrift from its old moorings, and sent you on a course of thought, which might or might not lead to a more desirable harbour. While we dine together, you shall tell me where you have passed these two years, or three, is it not? and whether the gallant little schooner still floats as daintily as of old, or, like some of my most promising barks of policy, has struck and gone to pieces when just in sight of land."

"'The Ariel' and I are both in good sailing trim, thank you, Signor Giuseppe, though we have parted company for a time. I remember you told me that you had once been elected a member of the 'Athenæum,' and suppose I have to thank that for the lucky chance which has brought you here to-night."

After dinner, as they were snugly ensconced in the smoking-room, the Italian said,

" My pipe will not scandalize the proprieties of your exclusive Travellers, I hope, caro Signore, by its Bohemian size and appearance. It is certainly less in harmony with our present surroundings, than with the rough quarters and red shirt of an Italian Volunteer Colonel; but it is an old friend, and has charmed away at various times many a fit of disgust at the failure of well laid plans, which no mere cigar would have had the power to dissipate."

As he spoke, Giuseppe filled and lighted a huge meerschaum pipe, coloured by long use to a deep mahogany tint, and capped with well worn silver, like that of a Heidelberg student, and with a few strong puffs kindled into the resemblance of a small furnace the enormous mass of tobacco which it contained.

" We have done much since 1860; my countrymen have learnt to realise that either in the south or north it is greater to be an Italian, than a Neapolitan, or Sicilian, a Lombard, or a Piedmontese."

"Yes," said Tresidder, "and they have also learnt that it is better to accept a practical monarchy under *Il*

Re Galantuomo than to let a generation slip by in vague aspirations for a Republic, possible only in theory."

"Possible, in fact no less, Signore Michael, as I believe, but it is the man that is wanting not the system. All revolutionary epochs depend for their event upon the character of the master-mind, they may happen to bring to the front. I am thoroughly loyal to Victor Emanuel, and welcome him as things go for the most desirable head of the State. But let the merits or demerits of a federal form of Government in other countries be what they may, I am not less, I am more than ever convinced, that an Italian Republic would have elements of stability which a Kingdom of Italy can never possess."

"From the differences of manners,

habits, and tone of thought, I suppose you mean, in the various provinces, and from their existing state of jealous rivalry with one another," replied Tresidder, "but will not the return of the capital to Rome settle all this? Naples may scorn to obey Florence, but both will surely give way readily enough to the old queen of the world."

"If there was any prospect of the romantic but degenerate and squalid mediæval town upon the Tiber becoming again by her own exertions anything which could at all resemble the old Imperial city, perhaps it might be as you suggest," answered Mola, "but that is absolutely impossible. The paralysing effect of the long continuance of the Papacy, as a temporal

power, is evident no less in the degenerate population than it is in the semi-
barbarous condition of the town itself.
A race of nobles who have no possession
but that of high sounding names, and
a populace who have only a liquid
dialect, and a graceful carriage, can,
in the almost entire absence of any
middle class of energetic traders, scarcely
hope to replace the ill-drained lanes
which are called streets, on the banks
of the Tiber, by anything which shall
rival the busy, well kept capitals of
modern times, and much less be able
to remind the world of her ancient
mistress.

"Why should Florence and Turin,
Genoa and Naples impoverish them-
selves to work their own effacement?
No, no, Rome has chosen to acquiesce

in a position of mere poetical interest
so long, that, for my part, I fear no
other *rôle* is possible for her. She
will do very well to play the part in
an Italian Confederation that Wash-
ington does in the United States of
America; but she can never attain,
again, the sort of supreme importance
held for instance here in England by
London. Without some such pre-emi-
nence, her position as the capital of a
kingdom, as the chief centre of a
monarchy, must be an absurdity."

Saying this with all the energy of
a mountaineer and a free thinker, Mola
rose and knocked the ashes from his
half-finished pipe, as if the discussion
of Italy, like the sound of a trumpet
to an old war-horse, had rendered
movement of some kind necessary.

Striding to the window, he watched silently for a few minutes the heavy clouds which, drifting up from behind the tall houses opposite on Carlton House Terrace, were rapidly changing the clear September moonlight into what might have been a dark night in cheerless November.

"If you have nothing to take you homeward immediately, forgive my warmth, Signor Tresidder, and walk with me some way towards my dwelling. I am quartered close to that towering American caravanserai, which to my foreign eye has turned your Portland Place from a dismal, even funereal avenue, into a noble street. The rain will hold off, I think, sufficiently long to enable you to get quietly back; and if I must confess,

caro mio, much as I respect and admire
the vigorous pulse which is throbbing
so lustily in this London of yours, I
cannot learn not to feel its outer aspect
as somewhat gloomy. In the day-time,
this sombreness is relieved by meeting
here and there with really fine buildings,
and by the perpetual bustle of your
active countrymen. But at night —
ah! at night, I like it not. If,
as often happens, I am sad, I
never willingly move in your streets
alone."

Tresidder laughingly consented to
accompany him, and after leaving Mola
at his lodgings in Langham Street,
turned back for his own hotel.

His road took him through Cavendish
Square, and while crossing it, he observed two figures, one of which was

apparently that of a man lying on the pavement, close to the two handsome houses in the centre of the north side, while the other, a woman, was bending over her companion, and trying to raise him.

He thought that it was in all likelihood nothing but one of the scenes, common enough in all English towns, where a wife is struggling to persuade some drunken brute of a husband to come home; but seeing no policeman near, and remembering the sad despairing faces of one or two poor creatures whom he had met similarly employed, he went towards the group, with the intention of helping the woman, if possible.

This was no case, however, of drunkenness, but of some really serious illness.

The man on the pavement was breathing
hard, or rather gasping, while the
woman had with difficulty contrived to
move him so as to support his head
upon the lowest step of the house-
door, and was loosening the handkerchief
from his neck, and throwing open his
shirt so that the night air might play
upon his chest.

He was evidently between sixty and
seventy years old, and might, when
young, have been handsome, as the
features, in spite of the drawn look
of pain and ghastly pallor which now
disfigured them, were without doubt
good and well marked, while the figure
was that of a powerful man, scarcely
less than six feet high.

There was something in the aspect
of the face, even in the condition in

which he first saw it, illumined by
the not very brilliant light of a London
gas-lamp; something also of grace in
the lines of the limbs as they lay
stretched on ´ the pavement, which at
once struck Tresidder as being out of
keeping with the dress—a workman's
much worn suit—and with the hands,
which, although somewhat delicate in
shape, were marked by evident traces
of severe labour of some manual
kind.

The woman, who was also clothed
very poorly, yet not without a certain
regard for neatness and propriety, resembled her companion so decidedly
in face, and was yet so many years
younger, being hardly more than two
or three and twenty, that there could
be little doubt as to the relationship

between them. The daughter's face wanted that indefinite air of something which is usually spoken of as good breeding, but ought to be called natural refinement, which characterised that of her father; but it amply redeemed the want by its greatly superior look of energy and power.

The contrast between the two faces, in this last respect, was of course more than usually noticeable, at this moment of the father's illness.

The woman turned a little from her charge to see who was approaching them, and the relieved expression of her countenance showed that she regarded the young man as a welcome assistant.

Michael stooped down and aided her efforts to restore her father to consciousness. Hearing her bewail the want of water, he remembered that he had passed, at the corner of the Square, the pump of a cab rank. Quickly running to the place, he filled a bucket and brought it back with him.

The girl, for she was scarcely more than that, thanked him with a rapid glance, and dipping both her hands in the water, sprinkled the face and throat of the sick man.

"Where do you live?" said Michael. "Your father ought to be taken home, and to have a doctor immediately. If it is far from here, let me get you a cab at once, for I see he is beginning to draw breath more easily, and may be strong enough to be moved in a few minutes."

"You are very kind," answered the girl, as she continued to soak her handkerchief in the cool water, and bathe her father's face. "I have no right to trouble you, and yet my father can, I fear, never to-night recover strength sufficiently to enable him to walk from here to our lodgings; and it will kill him to remain upon the stones. We live in Compton Street, a long way from here; and you, Sir, I daresay have never heard the name."

Tresidder, satisfied with this half permission, went off in search of a cab, and soon returning with one, made the girl seat herself in it first, and then he and the driver lifted up the poor fellow, and placed him by her side, so that she could fold her arms round him and let his head rest upon her breast.

Michael then mounted the box by the cabman, and thought, with some amusement, of his cousin Bertie's astonishment and disgust were he to meet him by daylight in such a situation.

A drive of about twenty minutes, brought them to the desolate street in Soho, to which the girl had directed him. No. 50 was not only their lodging, but that of as many different families as it contained rooms.

Michael and the driver unavoidably made some noise in carrying the poor old man, who, though much better, was scarcely yet conscious, up to the one room on the second floor, which was all they owned, and they

were saluted in forcible language by
the other lodgers, whose doors they
passed.

Tresidder, with the instinct of a
gentleman, had no sooner assisted the
daughter to place her father on the
bed—which, clean and neat, though
miserably old and scanty, was propped
up in one corner of the room—than
saying hurriedly that he would send
a doctor immediately, and would call
in the morning to hear how the sick
man progressed, he hastened away
before the girl had time to thank
him for his assistance.

After driving in the cab to the
house of a doctor in George Street,
Hanover Square, who, though a phy-
sician in large practice, happened to
be known to him by repute as always

ready to do additional work of a
charitable kind; and after obtaining
his ready promise to visit Compton
Street at once, Michael Tresidder
lighted a cigar, and as he walked
down at last to Dover Street, naturally
thought about his adventure and the
girl, whose courage and affection for
her father had been so noticeable.
He was the more interested from the
contrast which her tenderness presented to a certain look of hardness,
almost of fierceness, which spoilt a
countenance, both from its fairly good
features, and from its look of intelli-
gence, otherwise far from disagreeable.

CHAPTER V.

THAT'S right, Michael, you have come to time like a Briton," said a light man, in a shooting coat and knickerbockers of slate-coloured velveteen, who was standing on the Matfield platform as the train came in.

He was dark as a gipsy, with an olive complexion, and black moustache and imperial *à la* Vandyck ; but his merry brown eyes led you to suspect the presence of Irish blood in his veins.

"Out with you and your traps, or they will carry you on to York. Lord Ferndale has managed to get the express always to drop or pick up his passengers here; but the manager, or secretary, or whoever looks after such matters for the railway, is half-wild at being forced to break in upon the last fifty mile run, and bullies our station-master abominably if there is a minute's extra delay.

"That's your servant, I suppose, struggling to unearth some portmanteau. By Jove! he will not get them either, if I don't interfere."

Then, marching up to the scene of action, Bertie Cunninghame, with an entire change of tone, and his most languid air, addressed the bustling guard.

" Pray do not put yourself to any further inconvenience to find the Prince's luggage. Pray take it on to York; and perhaps you had better take his High-ness' gentleman, also. The special train that will have to bring them back may as well carry something besides one port-manteau and a gun-case."

" Are you really cracked at last, Bertie ?" said Michael, who had followed in time to hear the new rank his cousin had invented for him. " Surely half-a-crown would be as effectual, and in better morals."

" Hush, hush !" replied Cunninghame, with a wink; and as the gun-case was finally extricated, the relieved guard signalled hastily for the express train to move on.

"My dear fellow, you don't know the ways of the place as I do. Why, the Ferndales spent a fortune in tips, and yet their guests, especially old ladies, were always arriving or departing in a mutilated state (I mean as to boxes or lapdogs), until by good luck an Austrian Prince came down to Healey Towers, and being accustomed to politeness, was deposited at Matfield without even a wrapper or an umbrella.

"Lord Ferndale was furious, and remonstrated so strongly with the directors of the Railway Company, that they wigged their officials all round pretty handsomely. Since then I have always intended to work the Prince at a crisis, and you see it has answered."

"Much obliged, I am sure, for my

share in the transaction. A pretty fool I shall look on the way up to town if the same guard happens to be on duty, and takes his revenge by perpetually bowing and calling me His Highness before a lot of other people."

" Don't lament as to the future, Michael, but be properly grateful for the present.

" Well, old fellow, I am infinitely glad to see you; but come along, for young Robert Ellerton has been waiting in the dog-cart outside all this while, and neither he nor the horse are very fond of standing still. We could not bring a groom, as there would not have been room for your man."

Robert Ellerton turned out to be a good-looking youngster of eighteen or thereabouts; very like his elder brother in the outline of his face; but being very small and slight, he seemed more like an Eton or Harrow boy of fourteen, than the six months' old Guardsman he really was.

His appearance had gained him the nickname of " Fanny " in the Grenadiers; but like many other young men with sweet childish faces, he was famous for his pluck and skill in all active sports. The best racquet player of his time, and a member of the Harrow Eleven, he was also one of the straightest riders to hounds in the North Riding, and had nothing effeminate about him except his size and complexion, his smooth cheeks, and his long eyelashes.

After a drive of some seven or eight

miles, they came in sight of Healey
Towers as they were descending a hill
with a small town capped by a white
church-spire, and a wideish river at the
bottom. Some two miles on the other side
of this town, or large village of Healey,
the well-wooded country rose in bold
undulations from the valley. On the
summit of one of these hills, but backed
by grand old trees, and by a further
rise of the park beyond, was Lord
Ferndale's house, a large castellated
building, to which the numerous towers
had either given it the name, or had
been added to justify it.

From the highest of these, which
was round, and had a turreted porch
projecting from its base, a flag had
been floating when Tresidder first caught
sight of the house; but this was soon

lowered as the sun sank behind a wide
stretch of deep blue purple moorland
in the extreme distance.

The Castle — for we may as well
adopt the title by which its neighbours,
though not its owners, always spoke
of it—stood on a kind of plateau, and
an open space of green sward descended
from this until lost among the trees of
the park, or hidden by those of the
middle distance.

Passing through the town, in the
square market-place of which some com-
panies of Riflemen were now being
drilled, as the old Healey Volunteers
used to be during the long period of
panic which the First Napoleon created
for England, they crossed another rapid
stream in the midst of some charmingly broken land, half-park, half-meadow;

and entering the deer-park by a quaint gateway at the foot of the rise on which the Castle stood, wound round this slope, and drew up under the porch, just as the first dressing-bell, at seven o'clock, rang out from a turret above the offices.

A herd of does, collected in the angle of the letter L, formed by the wings of the building, were startled by this new arrival on the scene, and scampering past them, much to the horse's dis-gust, crossed a small lake which lay in front of the southern range of window, and joined a herd of stags, whose antlers could just be seen among the trees on the hill beyond.

By the time Michael Tresidder found his way to the library, after dressing for dinner, most of the party, which was not large, were already assembled there.

Lady Ferndale, a handsome, aquiline matron, with a haughty look, came forward to welcome her son's nurse and companion very warmly; and while answering her questions about Lord Ellerton, his father also approached and introduced himself by a hearty shake of the hand.

Lord Ferndale was a good deal smaller in every way than his stately better half, and was evidently not a little in awe of her ladyship.

He was a popular kindly man, who made every one whom he or "my Lady" asked to Healey Towers, feel as much at their ease in a few minutes as some hosts do after a dozen visits, and at the same time was perfectly capable of asserting his dignity should it be necessary to do so. He was owner of a magnificent pack of fox-hounds, and frequently acted as hunts-man with his sons or other young men as whips; although the kennels and hunting establishment at his estate of Allerdale close by, were far too completely organised to render any such amateur workmanship a matter of necessity; and his son, "Fanny" Ellerton, had inherited from him the prettiest seat that was to be found North of the Pytchley.

Bertie Cunninghame himself invariably treated Lord Ferndale with a courteous, almost affectionate deference, very diffe-rent from his decidedly off-hand non-chalance to the rest of the world, whether Prince or Squire. This he had done, ever since that day eight or nine years ago when, scarcely more than a boy, he had made his first appearance at Healey, and the Earl had left half-a-dozen grandees, who had arrived at the time, to the care of the groom of the chambers, and himself good naturedly climbed up to the top story of a bachelor's wing— much to the dismay of a dilatory housemaid—in order to show the shy, (for even Bertie was shy at eighteen) youngster his room, and see that he was comfortably installed.

"My niece Margaret, of whom you have no doubt heard Ellerton speak," said Lady Ferndale, "has not yet appeared, but I will ask you to take care of her at dinner, as she will like to talk to you of George.

" The Cliffords you must know already, as they are almost neighbours of yours in the west; at least to us in Yorkshire, Cornwall and Devon get rather mixed together.

" There is Sir Henry talking to Robert, and his wife is sitting in that low chair, while Miss Clifford is the pretty girl in the mauve, with whom and my daughter, Lucy, on the sofa, Bertie is plotting mischief of some kind no doubt. If I tell you all the people, you will have nothing left to learn from Margaret, so I will leave you now to speak to Lord Sunderland, who wants much to know you."

As Lady Ferndale moved away, a tall fair-haired man, who had been leaning against the chimney piece talking to Lady Clifford came across the room, and addressed Michael.

"Ah! Mr. Tresidder, I have often wished to meet you, and had you been in England, should have asked you to come to me long since. You may have heard of Lord Sunderland from your mother; Lady Eveline was one of my very oldest friends, and, if you will not think me impertinent in saying so, was always my ideal of a noble and charming woman."

Michael Tresidder, in addition to the pleasure it always gave him to hear his mother alluded to with praise or affection, was touched and flattered by such warmth of expression from a man who was, at that time, perhaps, the most in fluential and powerful personage in England, and whom public opinion generally blamed only for too great coldness of manner.

Edward Lascelles, fifteenth Earl and thirteenth Marquis of Sunderland, sprang from one of the six or seven really illustrious families that are even yet to be found among the nobles of Great Britain. It was impossible to study any particular epoch of English history without coming across some one or other of his ancestors. They had not certainly been as conspicuous, as some of their more ephemeral rivals, for their sweet taste in embroidered jerkins, at the time when many a courtier sowed the cost of fitting out a regiment of horse upon his cloak or his coat-sleeve, or for their ingenuity in devising masquerades like that of Leicester at Kenilworth; but they had spared neither their purses nor their persons in any cause which had appealed to their sense of patriotism and honour.

The present Marquis had succeeded to his title early in life, but was still at nearly sixty a bachelor, and from his enormous wealth, no less than from his great reputation, would have been the coveted spoil, in spite of his age, of many a high-born damsel's fashionable campaign, had not their lady-mothers long since learnt to teach them that any attempt to capture this particularly desirable but particularly cautious victim would be made in vain.

After his interview with the great
Statesman, Tresidder was much surprised to see in the recess of a
bay window his old Italian friend
Giuseppe Mola, in earnest conversation with a Mr. Beaumont, whom
Michael knew slightly, and who was
a devotee of painting and art of
all kinds.

This gentleman, like many virtuous
possessors of real taste but of much
capricious prejudice, admired everything that was beautiful so long
as it did not originate in his own
country, and took pains to draw
out and entertain, as he could do
very agreeably, almost every person
whom he met in society so long
as he was not an Englishman.

Michael wondered what accident

had brought Mola and himself together again so soon, and caused
that ardent republican to be a
guest of Lord Ferndale, who, though
generous and liberal in hospitality
as in all else, was a staunch Tory
and believer in the divine right of
Kings.

Tresidder was hastily crossing the
room to question his friend when
dinner was announced, and at the
same moment a side door opened,
and a girl entered, whom, from
her likeness to a photograph which
Ellerton had shown him, he knew
at once must be his friend Lord
Ellerton's betrothed, Lady Margaret
Charteris. Certainly she was beautiful.
Rich masses of soft rippling hair
swept back, in the present char-

ming fashion, in golden waves from above a broad white forehead. They left each delicate ear fully exposed, and were partly twisted into great broad plaits at the back of the small high-bred head, and partly allowed to fall in one very large loose curl which coiled lovingly round a smooth dimpled shoulder, and a neck and bosom with all the purity, but none of the coldness of marble.

Her slight and rather tall figure, exquisitely rounded, and falling with each movement into some fresh curve of graceful beauty, was enveloped in a cloud of transparent white gauze. This was looped up here and there by the bright crimson and starlike leaves of the point-settia, and allowing the light occasionally to play upon the folds of glistening satin, of which the under fabric of the dress was composed. A small bunch of the same brilliant leaves clustered in front of the dress, and one or two sprays were twined with a string of amber beads in her hair. Several rows of the same beads, but of a larger size formed a necklace, and others coiled round her arms.

Lady Margaret was fond of arraying herself in colours, that most fair beauties consider to be unbecoming; but Tresidder never learnt to attribute the charming effect produced to the extreme delicacy and transparency of her complexion, so much as in strictly æsthetic criticism he ought, perhaps, to have done; since, while in her presence it was difficult to turn his eyes from the sweet countenance. Her eyebrows were lightly pencilled, and like the long lashes which shaded the blue eyes, were of a lovely golden brown, a few shades darker than her hair, while her small, sharply-chiselled nose and chin, the contour of her cheeks, and of her loving, saucy lips, were more perfect in form than those of a statue ; but the real charm— as Tresidder soon came to know—was the constant play and endless variety of expression which characterised the face.

Now grave, now gay, at one moment pleading, at another defiant ; each mood seemed to pass as rapidly as clouds across the sky on a breezy summer day, but each, while it lasted, was so perfect, that it was difficult not to long that each successive phase might remain as the permanent expression.

In the course of dinner, both Lady Ferndale and her beautiful niece asked Tressider many questions about Lord Ellerton's illness and recovery; but if he had not remembered his friend's words, he would have been much surprised to find the young lady speak of the man, to whom she was to be married very shortly, in the open matter-of-fact tone of a familiar acquaintance, rather than with any of the shy coyness of a girl in love.

"When do you expect your yacht home, Mr. Tresidder?" said Lady Margaret in the course of dinner, "she must be a charming little ship; and we will come and cruize with you next summer, if you do not scorn lady-passengers."

" The ' Ariel' will be immensely honoured by your presence, Lady Margaret," replied Michael ; " and shall have a new set of sails before next season, to be more worthy of you. I do not know when to expect her exactly; perhaps Ellerton will like to bring her home himself, as he seems to have taken a fancy to sailing. His military business will not occupy much time, after they return to Malta. It is sometimes hard enough to get into a profession, but there is seldom much difficulty in getting out of one, and he gave notice of his intention to sell many months since."

" If George does come home in the

'Ariel,' Mr. Tresidder," remarked Lady Ferndale, "I hope, for my sake, as well as his, that his knowledge of navigation has improved since two years ago, when he nearly drowned us all upon a sandbank in the Solent."

Michael recalled some of Lord Ellerton's attempts to steer the schooner while lying upon the deck in a run across the Bay of Naples, and smiled as he said—

"Oh! there is no fear, Captain Harris is devoted to George, but still more enamoured of his own safety, and will soon resume the command of his ship, if he sees there is any chance of her getting into trouble."

As he spoke, he heard Lady Mar-

garet talking in very pure Italian
to her other neighbour, and turning
to compliment her on her accent,
learned, that as a little girl, she had
spent a winter in Genoa with the `
Ferndales, and been a pupil of Signor
Mola's, who had happened to be
there at the time, during one of
the many quiet vicissitudes of his
career.

"Those months have given me more t·
think of, than all the other years of
my life," she said, as she rose to
follow the other ladies from the room.
" Italy is, of all other countries,
the most likely to arouse a girl's
enthusiasm, since she has been so
great, and is so beautiful. We women
always follow impulse in our love of
one country, or hatred of another;

and as for politics, we are always
in extremes. I believe that I am
now something of an autocrat, but
I used to be a thorough Republican."
Slightly colouring at her own vehemence, Lady Margaret Charteris rose
and moved with the other ladies to
the door, and as Tresidder held it
open for her to pass, it was difficult for both Mola and himself to
suppress the united glance of ad-
miration which her singular grace
and beauty aroused.

CHAPTER VI.

WHILE Michael Tresidder, full of health and high spirits, is shooting in the well stocked preserves of Healey Towers, or riding with a merry party upon the fresh Yorkshire Downs, Nicholas Turnwell, the old man to whom he had played the part of a good Samaritan on that first night in England, was endeavouring to rally from his severe stroke of paralysis as quickly as the smoke and foul air of a murky London street would permit.

The extreme weakness which had brought on the seizure, and laid him in a dead faint upon the pavement of Cavendish Square, was due to insufficient food almost as much as to actual disease.

Turnwell had resembled very many of the forlorn inhabitants of London, the haggard men and women who cling to the inner edge of the footpath, as if the shadow of the houses could in some degree hide their poverty from the searching daylight; or who flit by us, perhaps, in the evening, and disappear out of the warm lamp glow into the dark archway of some crowded court.

He, like most of them, had not been

always poor, but had struggled with
the world, not without success, until
his health began to fail as years grew
on him. Philip, his son, had long
since reached an age at which he
might with ease have made his father's
life comfortable, if he had not spent
in dissipation the liberal salary which
he earned as a clerk in the house of
a great legal firm.

The only daughter was called Ruth;
and her tender care, and the contrast it presented to her stern and
shrewd face, we have already seen.
This woman's character had hardened
more from the fierceness of the battle
with adversity, which circumstances had
lately forced upon her, than from any
natural want of gentle feeling. Of this,

her treatment of the old man was sufficient evidence.

While sitting now by his bedside, and fondling his shrunken fingers in her own, scarcely less thin, but still womanly - looking hands, there came, now and again, a bright glimmer into her grey eyes, which had power to soften the expression of her features, as much as had the gleam of Autumn sunset, which played at this moment upon his head, to warm her father's hollow cheeks into a glow of apparent health.

" I wish Philip would come back, Ruth," said the sick man. " It is now many months since he has been to see us, and yet he must have observed that my strength was then failing rapidly, and not likely to re-

turn. It is hard to die and leave you
with no better protection."

" Do not let us talk of Philip,
father," interrupted Ruth; " tell me of
the happy days when my mother was
alive, and you lived in the pretty cottage at Hampstead. I can remember
the little garden looking over the
Heath right away to Barnet, and to
Harrow-on-the-Hill. Or tell me of your
own youth. Do not think of dying;
you are greatly stronger to-day than
you were yesterday. And as for me,
dear father, I am brave enough to
fight the world alone, if the worst
does come!"

Then in a lower tone, and with a
fierce look, strangely at variance with
that she had turned on the sick
man, she continued :

" Aye, and to fight Philip too, if he attempts to treat me as he treats poor father here. It is for his sake only that I bear it quietly now."

" That young man who helped you the night I was so troublesome, Ruth, has not been here again, has he ?" said Nicholas; and as he spoke, his hand clutched nervously at a black despatch - box, which lay on a small table close to the head of the bed, and between it and the wall.

" No, father ; not since the next morning. You looked so worried and anxious when I told you about him, and read his name from the card he had given me, that I would not let him in when he called to inquire. Indeed, you were sleeping at the time.

But there was something in his face I liked, and which did not seem as if he would have thought meanly of us for being poor. I fear that I answered him churlishly—at least that Mr. Tresidder thought so, and considered that my tone was meant to show him that he was scarcely welcome."

"A kindly, pleasant face had he, this Michael (you called him Michael, did you not?) Tresidder. Well, I am glad of it, for the sake of the people of Portruan. I have never spoken, even to you, Ruth, about my boyhood, nor of anything earlier than the Hampstead cottage, which you remember; and your mother died too early to tell you much.

"We were not originally Londoners; we came from the north of Cornwall

—indeed, only left it when we married; and I know every nook in young Tresidder's house, and every wood and field on his estate as well, aye, better than I know each corner in this small room. That is, I remember them as they were thirty years ago. No doubt they are altered now."

When speaking of these memories of his youth, Nicholas Turnwell's countenance gained a look of dignity and of firmness, most unlike its usual expression, and as it did so, the air of refinement, which was always noticeable, as we have said, became most strongly marked.

"Kind and pleasant," he continued, half repeating his former words. "Yes, it is easy to be both, as well as to wear the appearance of them, when one's whole existence has been continually surrounded with all the material happiness wealth and station can give."

Then, after a short silence, he said :

" Philip's face is very different ; but do you not think, Ruth, that if he had grown up at Portruan, he might have rivalled this young Tresidder?"

" Philip would have been handsomer, father, I grant you; indeed, he almost is so now, for his features in themselves are better and more decided. But in disposition, my brother would not have been less heartless if he had been brought up in a palace. Had he been rich, he would have only added pride to his other vices, and would have tyrannised over all who were in any way within his power."

Ruth spoke these words with a bitterness which was half sad, half fierce; and then looking at an old-fashioned gold hunting - watch which was ticking loudly on the table, as if remonstrating against the incongruously mean surroundings amongst which it found itself, she continued in the tone with which she generally addressed her father:

" It is half-past six o'clock, I see; and I have to be at Exeter Hall ten minutes before seven o'clock. Let me give you your medicine; and then if I put the tea-things within your reach, and leave you matches, so that you can light the night-lamp, and boil the water in this little kettle over it when you like — you will be able to take care of yourself, dear father, will you not, until my return?"

She made all these little preparations as she spoke, and then coming back to his bedside, said :

" I will put a string on the latch, so that you can open the door if you wish ; but no one can get in otherwise. If you should feel that you want help, rap with this stick upon the floor. Mrs. Barham, who lodges in the room below, is a good soul, and would be pleased to come to you."

Having smoothed the pillows of the bed, given Nicholas his medicine, and made all these other arrangements for the poor invalid's comfort in her absence, Ruth Turnwell went to put on her own bonnet and cloak behind the old curtain which was stretched as a screen across one corner of the room, and concealed her little pallet-bed and a small space for dressing.

Shortly returning, however, she knelt down by the bedside, and throwing her arms round her father, kissed him several times.

The old man fully returned her affection, and as the girl was leaving the room, said with solemn earnestness :

" May the great God bless you for your kindness, Ruth darling, and protect you now and always. Good-bye, dear one. I shall be quite happy for an hour or two."

AN old violin case lay by Turnwell's bedside upon the same table as the little black despatch box, and soon after the sound of the girl's step had died away upon the stairs, he opened it and took out a well-worn and dark-coloured violin, which he handled with the peculiar loving touch never used except by those whose deep appreciation of its music gives them an almost idolatrous veneration for the instrument itself.

After playing softly a few old tunes
and making the strings speak in some
low plaintive chords, like whispered
recollections of the past, Nicholas Turnwell evidently allowed himself to follow
the suggestion of his own music, and
wander in imagination back to the
scenes of his distant youth. Sharply
and vividly he remembered how—upon
one night, long, very long ago—after
a rapid ride of nearly two hours, he
had reached one of the small villages,
or rather hamlets, which are scattered
here and there without apparent reason
on the swelling Cornish hills, and had
tapped vigorously with his hunting
whip at the door of one of the larger
cottages which seemed, by its size,
to be a road-side inn.

It had been some time before he

could arouse the old couple who kept the house; but at length an upstairs window had creaked open cautiously, and a shrill, frightened voice called through the darkness to know who was there. Upon his answering—

" Do not be afraid, Mrs. Hawker, it is only I. I am sorry to disturb you so late, but I must please have shelter for the night, and I want to leave my horse with you till the morning."

She had called back to her husband inside—

" Why, John, 'tis the young Squire, sure enough; do ye get up and let him in, 'tis a terrible night for the likes of he to be skeering about the country."

After this aside—she had shouted down loudly to him :

"John be coming, Sir; he won't be a brave while getting on his clothes; and your own room is quite ready."

Lights had appeared, and very shortly the door had been opened by an old man, with a lantern, who touched his grey forelock as he came to hold the horse's bridle. Nicholas could, in his musing, hear his own voice again, saying—

"Put him up somewhere for the night, John, and in the morning get a lad to take him home; and now, Mrs. Hawker, all I want is a candle, as I have to be off very early to-morrow."

"Sure, Master Nicholas, you be never going away from home on Christmas Day," had remonstrated the old woman, giving him, however, the candle as she spoke, for she had already noticed the determined look of his face.

Once more, in fancy, he entered the room, which he used to keep at the cottage, and changed his hunting clothes for a half sailor, half artist suit; and once more he seemed to spend the night in wandering up and down, or in putting a few clothes together in a small knapsack. Then, as soon as the morning broke, he seemed again to write a message that his horse should be taken home, and leaving the paper on his table, to let himself out, and start with his knapsack for a ten mile walk to a small seaport town.

He remembered well the fishing boats

which, when he had reached the place, were just starting for their day's work; and how, though he was entirely unknown to them, it had been no difficult matter to persuade the crew of one to go a little out of their ordinary beat, and land him at Trebarwith Strand. He saw again the great frowning precipices of slate, some coal-black, others varying through every shade of brown and grey, which there enclose an exquisite stretch of firm sand, while as the boat approached, he passed again some little distance out to sea under the isolated Gull Rock. On the shore he now saw again the only habitation, a low, stone-roofed, granite-chimneyed dwelling, with small lattice windows, and deep porch.

Some attempt had apparently been

made to cultivate a few evergreens
under the shelter, even to coax them
to climb up the walls, but the winter
storms were too fierce to allow of much
success.

He fancied now, as he did on that
Christmas morning, that he could see
at the window of this cottage the pretty
young widow, who with a little country
maid was its only tenant, as she
was standing, after breakfast, at the
window of her small sitting-room, and
looking wistfully seaward. He thought
of her history. Her father had been a
clergyman, and came of a good race,
but they were very poor, and when
five years before, Ellen had fallen in love
with—though he was some years older
than herself—and married the still
handsome sailor Richard Borlase, who

had worked his way up to the owner-
ship of one or two small coasting
vessels, she had met with little opposition from the scruples of family pride.

Eighteen months after the marriage,
her husband had been tempted to earn
more for his wife, by undertaking a
distant voyage, which promised great
profit. Unfortunately, a great storm had
overtaken him on the coast of Africa,
and for three years and a half Ellen
had lived a widow in this lonely cottage.

As in his waking dream the boat rounds
the headland west of the cove, the morning being quiet and the sea calmed by
the long rain, he can again see her hurry
out, while her eyes brighten, as the boat
runs close enough to a projecting bed
of rocks for him to jump out, and then

pushes off again to the open sea. Before she has half crossed the smooth white sand to meet him, he has met her and throwing his arm round her waist, has cried,

"A happy Christmas to you, my sweet Ellen, you did not expect me yet; but I have come to claim my bride sooner than I thought possible. How lucky that we have already had our banns called these last three Sundays."

Ellen had coloured painfully, and half withdrawn herself from his embrace as she had remonstrated shyly—he could still hear her now, oh! so plainly—

"Oh, Nicholas dear, do you really want to marry me at once? I cannot leave my quiet nook so easily. Besides, I do not know what you wish to do

with me," she had added, smiling
archly.

"Do with you, my pretty one?" he
seemed to repeat again, "we will go
to the great city, and if we do not make
our fortune, we will at least make each
other's happiness. As to hurry, one
cannot have a good thing too soon;
and since you have been so rash as to
trust your heart to me, why you may
as well give your whole self to my keeping at once."

It had not been hard for him to persuade his love, that what both wished
could be easily and wisely accomplished.

After breakfast, while she put a few
things together, he had walked to a
neighbouring village to get some kind
of conveyance, and arrange with the

clergyman for the marriage to take place that morning.

There had been no bridal trousseau to be waited for; no friends of love, and friends of conventionality to be warned and to be invited; not even a wedding cake to be made.

Thirty years ago, clergymen in the far West were accustomed to take things easily. So long as the fee was paid, the ceremony of marriage or of funeral was easily performed, and few questions were asked; fewer need have been answered.

The chief witness had been the clerk, who also gave Ellen to her husband; the only attendant had been the little maiden from Trebarwith.

Once more he seemed to be journeying in the crazy four-wheel trap, which, under the guidance of a rough labourer, had carried his bride and himself to meet the Exeter coach that afternoon at Camelford. And as he seemed again to wrap his little wife up for the long winter's ride, he could still feel her caress, still hear her whisper—

"Dear, dear husband, I am so very happy."

His remembrances became more sad. For a long time after his marriage he had gone on prospering humbly in the world; had become a master printer, and had employed a great number of hands at one of those singular places of business at the back of Fleet Street: but, little by little, his trade had begun about fifteen years since to fall off, and other firms to obtain the orders which used to come to his house in Garrett Court.

Possibly, as he now sadly reflected, his own somewhat irresolute disposition might have prevented his exercising the authority necessary for the management of a large concern. Possibly, he had failed from lack of the capital sufficient to keep up with the continued improvement in type, machinery, and other appurtenances of the printing trade.

But, be this as it may, instead of a source of income, the affair came at last to be a considerable weekly loss; and he had been at length compelled, though at the expense of his pretty Hampstead cottage, he struggled hard to tide over in the hope of better times, to give up business on his own account and accept the post of foreman under another master.

Before many years his health had begun to fail, and this post also had to be relinquished. Since that time he had, for the last four years, been employed as a reader, *i.e.*, to read over and correct the proofs as they were set up by the compositors, at the office of an evening newspaper.

His good education, and the considerable knowledge he possessed of general literature, had fitted him for this occupation, and as no night work was required, he had been, until the last few months, able to attend to his duties regularly.

Since that time he had been obliged to absent himself, at first perhaps

only for one day occasionally; then, by
degrees, for two or three in every
week; and now he had not been able
to go to his work at all, since the
night of his seizure.

He thought, with gratitude, that the
staff of the newspaper had frequently
subscribed to help him a little; but now
he had been entirely abandoned by his
son for the last six months, and depended
upon his own scanty earnings merely,
and upon those of his daughter Ruth.

The thought of his son was very bitter. With an expression of remorse, he
roused himself from his long musing, and
let the violin, which he had hitherto
held, fall from his hands upon the bed, on
which the open case was also lying.

Then drawing a small key, attached
to a black ribbon, from under his

pillow, he unlocked the despatch box, standing on the table at his head, and took out the bundle of old letters, which was all it contained.

At the top of the packet was an envelope larger than the rest, and as the string which bound them together was untied, and these latter fell from the old man's weak fingers, some slipping to the floor, some being arrested by the bed-clothes, he managed to retain the former one. It was directed in a bold running hand, although the colour of the ink was much faded by time, to

Nicholas Turnwell,
　　At the Bull and Mouth Inn,
　　　　Holborn,
　　　　　London,

and bore the postmark of a Cornish town.

Drawing the enclosures from this, and unfolding one of them—while the other, a mere strip of paper, fluttered down and happened to fall through the holes in the violin—he read with a strange mist gathering in his eyes, the following words, written in the same decided characters as was the address :—

"Nicholas Turnwell,

"I write to you by the name, which you tell me you have adopted, as the act being accomplished, which you have persisted in performing contrary to my express commands, it is impossible for me to consider you any longer as my son.

"Although you have chosen by this marriage to degrade the position to which you were born, I am willing to believe that you have still some of the feelings of a gentleman, and as such I hold you to your promise. You have assured me, that strange as I cannot but think it after your conduct, you still hold the honour of my family and myself in some esteem, and you have given me your word that you will never resume my name, that you will never divulge to your children, should you have any, nor allow your wife to do so, your connection with me, and that you will never put forward your claim to the succession to my property.

"By carrying out these obligations faithfully, you can make the only reparation now in your power to the father you have disobeyed, and the family you have disgraced.

" As this is the last communication which will ever pass between us, and as I do not wish you to disgrace us still further by starving, I enclose a draft for five thousand pounds. In the sphere of life, which you have chosen to prefer to that wherein you were born, this sum will be sufficient to enable you to start with respectability.

" ARTHUR TRESIDDER.

" Portruan Manor,
" February 4th, 1830."

At the foot of this letter was written in pencil, and scarcely legible—

" The five thousand pounds returned the same day as received, with these words : The promise shall be kept.

" H. T."

It was little wonder that the sacrifice of natural affection to family pride, which spoke through every line of Arthur Tresidder's letter, should now, after the lapse of nearly five-and-thirty years, still exercise a terrible effect upon the mind of the son to whom it was addressed, especially when, as now, his whole strength was prostrated by illness.

Nicholas Turnwell, for we may as well continue to respect the secret which its victim has kept with such constant resolution during all these years, missed no word and seemed able to spare himself not one drop of the venom that each contained; but as he read, his face grew ghastly pale, while the pupils of his eyes appeared to increase in size, as they became more and more intently fixed upon the paper.

When he had finished the letter, drops of clammy perspiration had gathered on his forehead, and while he was endeavouring, with trembling fingers, to fold and return it to the envelope, a fearful change came over his features, like that which had preceded the former seizure, and had given Ruth perhaps even a greater feeling of anxiety and horror than the subsequent loss of consciousness.

The poor man made a desperate effort. He tried to reach the stick, which would summon Mrs. Barham, the lodger on the floor below, to his aid; but his elbow knocked it from its place as he moved his arm, and it fell, not, unfortunately, with a sharp noise upon the floor, but silently, out of his reach, on a cloak, which had slipped down from behind him a few minutes before. The failure of this attempt, and the effort it had caused him to make, took away the last remnant of the poor man's strength; and he fell back aslant upon his pillow, so that his head went beyond it, and instead of meeting the support which was essential to give him any chance of recovering breath, drooped over the bedside.

For a moment the lips moved, and seemed to frame the words, "Ruth, poor Ruth!" but scarcely any sound was audible. After that, the same complete unconsciousness ensued which had overcome him in Cavendish Square. But there was now, and for nearly another two hours there could be, no brave daughter at hand to help him back to life.

Before half of that time had elapsed, Nicholas Turnwell had passed beyond the reach of all assistance, and had freed himself by death from the promise, made possibly in hasty pride, but adhered to with noble fidelity throughout all the trials of his life.

E must return to his daughter, Ruth, who hurried out of Exeter Hall, as soon as the concert was finished, and hastened up Drury Lane, full of anxiety for her father.

As she passed the portico of the theatre, a knot of dissipated looking young men happened to come out from the centre doors; and one of them, catching sight of the girl, put his

arm round her waist and cried out in
mocking tones.

" Well met, my amiable sister, what
brings you here at night? I thought
you were always so well employed in
keeping the old man company."

The speaker was Philip Turnwell. He
was physically a handsome man of
about seven-and-twenty years of age,
but there was an evil look about the
eyes, and his face bore signs of a fast,
intemperate life.

The cheeks were smooth-shaven, and
this and the black moustache, which
he wore twisted up at the ends, gave
him something of the appearance of an
actor, while in figure he was tall and
well made. His sister freed herself from
his embrace with a look of disgust, and
said, in a hard, cold voice,

"You have been drinking, as usual, Philip, yet for once I am glad to see you, for only two hours ago poor father was asking for you. Had you been near us during the last six months, you would have known that he has been very ill—that he is dying. But I suppose, if you care about it at all, you are only glad to hear that he cannot be, even the slight trouble you have ever allowed him to be to you, much longer."

Ruth Turnwell was turning to walk rapidly away, when her brother, who had seemed half-shocked at, half-incredulous of her words, seized her arm, and said,

"My father has not done much for me, why should I burden myself with him? besides, I daresay he is not worse than usual."

"Be silent, Philip, or the very houses will fall down to crush you for such unnatural words. I tell you that he is dying, that he was nearly dead four days ago, and that he may at any moment have a return of the fit of paralysis which struck him then. And you can treat it almost as a jest, you, who have killed him, for good food might have prevented his illness, or at least staved it off for a time. But why do I waste time in speaking to a heartless drunkard, whose wine, perhaps, only tastes the sweeter that it has helped to build his father's grave."

As she thus spoke she dashed away his hand from her arm, and run from him beyond the steps of the theatre.

Philip Turnwell furious at her

taunting words, raised his other hand
as if to strike her; but his sister
had already escaped, and was half
way across Russell Street, ere the blow
could descend.

With a muttered curse he was
turning to rejoin his companions, when
some touch of natural feeling seemed
to come over him, and he called after
her, "Ruth, Ruth, stop and tell me
more." The girl, however, would not
pay attention; indeed, in the noise of
the crowded street, and as she was
running quickly she might not have
heard his call. Again for a moment
he appeared to hesitate, but the better
impulse once more conquered, and he
dashed across the street, between the
carriages and cabs, waiting for the
visitors at the Opera House as well as

at Drury Lane Theatre, in time to catch the girl before she had reached Long Acre. As she heard his step behind her, Ruth Turnwell turned and saw from the expression of Philip's face, that her news had really touched him for the time at least. So great, however, was the horror she felt for the brother whom she really considered, as she had told him, accountable for their father's past wretchedness and present danger, that she could not trust herself to say more than, "Come, see for yourself, how far I speak the truth," without in any degree slackening the rapid pace at which she was proceeding.

Together, but without further attempt at conversation, they threaded the labyrinth of dingy thoroughfares which lie south-west of Soho Square, and before long reached the lodgings in Compton Street. In the darkness it was somewhat difficult to grope along the passage and find the foot of the dilapidated staircase; but Ruth here, for the first time, touched her brother's hand and guided him. As they ascended the second flight, she was terrified at not seeing a light from her father's room shining through the crevice under the ill fitting door, since he was in the habit of lighting his own candle, when the twilight faded, with the matches purposely left on his table.

In hope, however, that the sick man had only dozed off earlier than usual, the girl whispered "Hush," and opening the door silently stole very quietly towards the bed.

Before she had crossed half the room, small as it was, the faint glare of the street lamps through the uncurtained windows, showed the figure of her father lying as he had fallen when the fit seized him. In horror at his position, Ruth rushed to his head and strove to raise it. As she did so, the cold chill, which met her touch, and the terrible weight, left no doubt that the father she had loved with such faithful care was dead, and had been dead some time.

This girl's life had distorted so much of the natural softness of a woman's disposition, that her first feeling was not the sorrow of a daughter, but the fierce rage of a tigress robbed of her young. Starting up, she sprang towards her brother, and with the words

"Monster! your work is done," seemed about to tear at him with her outstretched hands; but in another instant her grief conquered her anger, and turning back she fell on her knees by the bedside, and throwing her arms round the body of Nicholas Turnwell sobbed as if her heart would break.

Bad as Philip was, he had not possibly arrived at the extreme pitch of cruelty, that would have allowed him to recognise to himself the fact that his father was dangerously ill, and yet to continue his course of utter neglect.

He simply had never given the old man a thought, and now, for the first time, he realised the desperate condition to which he had sunk, and the little cost to himself, at which his condition might have been improved, and probably the frightful circumstances, which were the immediate cause of death, obviated. He was greatly shocked, and as he looked at the bed with its fearful burthen, and heard his sister's violent sobs, years that had been long forgotten crowded into his mind. They brought back to him memories of happy childish play with an indulgent father, who grudged no trouble that could procure for his son such pleasure as their means would allow. They reminded him of the merry, laughing child-sister, whose baby footsteps he had helped to guide, and who, as she grew a year or two older, loved him with all the affection of a tiny girl for a big boy-brother.

Midnight pleasures, and the dissolute

existence of a fast man about town,
had substituted for these recollections
the present facts. The indulgent father
dead, in want, and in misery, as to
which he, the son, had not even cared
to inquire : while the once-loving sister
did not hesitate to accuse him of the
murder.

As he felt about for the matches on
the table with that sensation of awe
in the presence of death, which men,
whose nervous system is weakened by
the habit of drinking, feel at all times
to an extraordinary degree, aggravated
by such thoughts as these, Philip Turnwell resolved to redeem some, at least,
of the past. The dead father was beyond recall, but the sister was more
than ever in need of his protection,
and by fulfilling his duty to her, he

might yet recover some portion of her love. It is easier, however, to feel the momentary impulse sufficient to form good resolutions, than to achieve that constant mastery over degraded passions, which may be necessary to keep them.

The matches were at last found, and as the light of the candle fell upon the gold hunting-watch upon the table, this pitiful fellow could not resist a feeling of pleasure that the handsome trinket, which he had often coveted, was now his own. Excusing his action to himself, by the pretence that he could not disturb his sister in order to look at the dead man's face. Philip, instead of attempting to do so, took up the watch and examined it. On the back was engraved a coat of arms,

and the three goats' heads in the
shield seemed to remind him of a
seal he had lately handled, but he
could not exactly remember where or
when.

While trying to recall these particulars, his eyes happened to fall upon
the letters scattered upon the floor and
the bed, and upon the direction of one,
which chanced to be turned towards
him, he read—

Nicholas Tresidder, Esq.

Instantly it flashed into his memory,
that this was the name with which the
bearings on the coat of arms were
connected, and that he had seen both
in a deed, which he had been employed
to copy at his office that very afternoon.

Philip's curiosity was now fully aroused to discover how his poor father had become possessed of a watch engraved with the arms, and of letters addressed in the name of the rich family, whose great position and large estates in Cornwall were widely known ; and whose present representative, Michael Tresidder, he had seen and greatly envied, when some few days back he had called as a client to see Mr. Townsend, one of the partners in his firm.

As her brother stooped to pick up the envelope he had noticed, Ruth, who had succeeded, in some degree, in controlling the first violence of her sorrow, rose, and turning to him said, as her hand still rested on the dead man's arm—

"This separates us for ever; I would deny your right to help in the burial of my poor father, whom you, his son, have murdered, did I suppose that you would care to insist on what would cost you money. That watch I see you have already begun to handle; take it, for its metal gives its value in your eyes. We had no other single thing which can interest you, because there is nothing but these few poor articles of furniture, which you could sell. They must go to pay for his funeral. Besides them, there are only a few personal relics, utterly worthless to you, which I must, I *will* keep."

Ruth's movement had disclosed the open letter lying on the bed near the hand, which had tried in vain to refold it, and as she spoke, Philip, whose eyes were very sharp, had, from where he first stood, read the signature of "Arthur Tresidder." On moving nearer he had made out the whole of the document ; his face lit up with an expression of triumph, and seizing the sheet, he cried—

"Keep all else you like, Ruth ; but all these letters are mine by law, and though I cannot understand them yet, I intend to take them home at once and examine their meaning."

As he spoke, he quickly gathered the rest of the scattered bundle up, so that his sister could not hinder him, and calling to her that he should return early in the morning, he hurried from the room, and out of the house, without bestowing further thought upon the dead man.

She was, of course, unable to com-
prehend the cause of his haste, but was
too much oppressed by the recent
shock she had received, and too glad
to be rid of her brother, of whom
the very sight was now almost more
than she could endure patiently, to
raise any objection to his going. On
the contrary, no sooner was he down
the staircase than she shut, locked, and
double locked the door to prevent any
possibility of his return; and then,
alone with the dead, performed the last
sad duties Nicholas Turnwell would ever
need at her hands.

After this, wearied out by her grief,
and being as yet too much absorbed
by it even to think of her own utter
loneliness in the world henceforth,
she threw herself upon her own bed,

and buried her face in the meagre pillow.

Nature, which is in youth so mercifully strong to make us forget all sorrow for a time, came to this poor girl's relief, and by degrees the convulsive sobs grew less violent and less frequent. She would awake before many hours to a future deprived of its only gleam of happiness; but for her solitary battle, she would have gathered some increase of strength from the troubled but still refreshing sleep which now overcame her.

Philip Turnwell carried the bundle of letters to his own lodgings in Essex Street, and had perused them every one before, as daylight was breaking, he went to bed. He was unable, however, to close his eyes; not because

he grieved for his dead father, but
owing to the deep excitement and
triumph which the story disclosed by
the letters, and the consequences in-
volved by it, had roused. It was clear
enough that the old man he had
treated with contemptuous neglect, was
by right no poor, struggling Nicholas
Turnwell, but was entitled to wealth
and position, as Tresidder of Portruan
Manor.

Philip remembered, from the recitals
in the deed which he had copied, that
the Arthur Tresidder whose words he
had just read, had died two-and-twenty
years ago; that the estates had been
entailed on his son Nicholas; but that
as at the time of the death that son
had not been heard of for more than
fifteen years, they had passed to the

distant cousin, Colonel Tresidder, and from him to the present possessor. He had not regretted his father's death much before, but he now gnashed his teeth with rage to think that the poor old man had lived nearly three years too long. For Philip was already lawyer enough to know, that a claim cannot be made with legal effect more than twenty years after the right to make it has accrued.

Suddenly a thought flashed across his mind, which made him start up in bed, and dash water from the jug, standing near, over his face, as if to insure that he was thoroughly awake, and that the golden vision, which had risen before his eyes was not a mere dream.

As heir to his father, merely, he

could not put forward a claim which Nicholas had allowed to die out by lapse of time. But was there not? Yes, there certainly was, not only a limitation of the Portruan estates to the son of Arthur Tresidder, but to that son's son.

Jumping up, he strode up and down the room, in frantic impatience for the full daylight to come and permit of his rushing to the office, and scanning that deed again. If he was right in this supposition, the lapse of twenty years, though it would have prevented Nicholas from claiming the life-estate to which he was entitled, had not affected his son's position to the value of a penny. He himself was in truth at this moment no longer Philip Turnwell, compelled

to earn a pitiful salary as a lawyer's
clerk, but Philip Tresidder, the actual
owner of property worth several thou-
sands a-year.

As it wanted yet some hours of
the period at which business begins,
he was obliged to control his impatient
desire to grasp what he saw thus
temptingly dangled before him. And
as he thought over the matter again
and again, so far as the long series
of letters from his grandfather to his
father, and his own recollections of that
deed revealed it, he recognised with
some dread the want of two or three
important links in the chain of evidence which must establish his rights—
for he would think of them by no other
name.

The man was cunning, rather than

clever ; and by the time he left his lodgings, had resolved to adopt without scruple a crooked and double-faced course for a little while, as being that which would be most likely to insure his eventual success. At the usual hour he was in attendance at his office, and asked only for a short leave of absence in the afternoon, on account of his father's death.

During the course of the morning, an excuse was easily found for a fresh examination of the deed connected with the Portruan property, and under pretence of verifying the recitals, of the older documents to which it alluded. It was difficult to hide the flush of triumph which spread over his face, when the original limitations proved to be in strict accordance with his supposition.

An estate, as is well known, can only be tied up so as to fix its descent upon one person not yet born at the time of settlement; but by an accident, three generations of Tresidders happened to have been in existence together fifty years ago. These were Joseph, the then Squire, his son Arthur, and his grandson Nicholas. The first of these three had settled the property by will in perfectly valid legal form; *i.e.*, upon Arthur for life, with remainder to Nicholas for his life, and with further remainder to Nicholas' eldest son, who might survive him, and have been born, of course, in lawful wedlock; but in the event of his, Nicholas, having no legitimate issue, all was to go to the distant cousin, Colonel Tresidder, and to his children.

By virtue, as we have said, of this last clause, Michael Tresidder was at present in possession, since his father had succeeded when, after long search, neither Nicholas nor any son of his could be found, and he was consequently supposed to be dead, and to have left no issue.

Philip Turnwell copied surreptitiously all this important portion of the will, and when his time for absence came, drove as fast as a hansom cab would carry him to a small court in Clement's Inn at the back of the Strand.

Here lived an intimate friend some few years older than himself, and who had gained a considerable reputation among low sporting men for his knowledge of all those intricate dodges, by which dishonesty of various kinds might be practised, and yet the strict letter of the law evaded.

Robert, or 'Spider,' Burrows, as he was generally called by his associates, knew that a visit at this hour must be a matter of real business, and, his own time being precious, stopped Philip's attempt to make any explanation, by saying—

"Hand up the papers; I had rather find out the case myself."

Turnwell gave him the bundle of letters and the extract from the will, but watched his treasures narrowly while out of his own custody.

After twenty minutes of careful study, making notes as he read, Burrows laid his hand upon the open pile, and burst out with an oath—

" By ——, Phil, it's uncommon well done. I knew you were sharp, but did not believe you had either skill or pluck enough for such a scheme as this."

" Confound your schemes!" retorted his client. " It's all true, every word of it. I had no more hand in writing those letters than you had, and had not set eyes upon them until last night."

Philip then related the manner of his father's death, and the discovery, and also his own investigations at the office since.

Burrows ceased to look incredulous, as he had done at first, but could not, nor indeed did he make any effort to repress his disgust.

"You precious blackguard! do you mean that you have spent all day in looking into this—which, if a good case at all, will be just as good to-morrow, or any other day for the next twenty years—and left your father's dead body without thought or care?"

"Oh, there's that sister of mine; she will have done all the needful long before this," answered Philip, care-lessly. "She is a deal better pleased not to have me, I can tell you."

"So I should suppose," said Burrows, with an expression of contempt, which he took no pains to conceal. "However, you being a brute is no affair of mine, and this may be. If what you tell me is true, and you have not really forged all these, it appears pretty clear that the gentry of Cornwall

have the honour to include your virtuous self among them.

"But you'll scarcely expect young
Michael Tresidder to give up without
a hard struggle. Eight or ten thousand
a year is worth fighting for. We shall
have to prove every line of our case.
First there's the question of iden-
tity. However, that's not so difficult,
if the letters are once admitted as
genuine.

"You must see if there are not
some more in Arthur Tresidder's writing
at the office and compare them; and
then your sister and yourself can prove
the finding. But there's a harder thing
to prove than all that, and you have
not a syllable of clue—your mother's
marriage, and your own birth. Unless
you are the legitimate son of Nicholas,

and his eldest son, too, mind, the whole affair goes utterly to smash.

"Keep quiet till we have found out a little more. You stay on at your office, and poke among all the family papers you can get sight of. I'll turn the matter over: I don't say but what the prospect is worth thinking about, but there is a deal to be done yet. Look in again, to-morrow, about this time; or stay, you cannot get leave again, so I'll come round to you in Essex Street to-morrow night, and we will talk 'it over. By that time I shall have hit upon a plan of action. Now I must see another man, who has been waiting this half-hour. Good-day. I must keep the papers."

Without much ceremony Burrows

then pushed Philip out at one door, while he rang for the clerk to show in the fresh client at another.

Turnwell went back to his own office rather less elated than when he left it, and rather uneasy at having left his papers; but he muttered to himself—

"I do believe Spider will act on the square with an old pall; and d—— it, there's a deal to be done yet. But, by Jove! the prospect *does* seem worth thinking about, even to him, and no mistake."

CHAPTER IX.

HAPPILY unconscious of the sword which was hanging over him, Michael Tresidder was enjoying thoroughly his visit at the Ferndale's pleasant house.

All such visits are much alike. The sport at Healey was perhaps rather better than at most places, but the people were much the same, the conversation was lively but not brilliant; while Lady Lucy Ellerton, Miss Clifford, and the other

young ladies only rode, played and sang,
as young ladies always do—prettily.   One
evening, however, Lady Margaret, who
had real musical talent, rendered with
much pathos and cultivated execution,
Beethoven's "Sonata Pathetica," and
scarcely had these last mournful chords
died away, when the fair player, calling
upon the other ladies to join in the chorus,
and turning with a bright smile to Mola,
who stood a few paces from her, struck up
in a rich contralto voice, the stirring march
or hymn, "Liamo Italiani," which the Gari-
baldians had adopted as their battle song.

The Italian joined in here and there,
with a mellow bass voice; but the flush
that passed over all of his pale face, which
the close beard allowed to be visible,
and the deep light which seemed to
kindle and glow in his dark eyes,

showed the extent to which the familiar music moved him. As the rest of the company applauded this spirited performance, he moved quietly up to the piano, and bending down as if to turn the leaves of the music, said, in a low voice,

"A thousand thanks, dear lady, for a pleasure so great as to be almost a pain. You ought to have been of my country, and would have helped us more than a thousand men." Then, in a louder tone, "You would scarcely believe, Miss Clifford, the degree to which we emotional Southerners are ex- cited by stirring music. I have seen a pair of common strolling lads, with but a flageolet and a crazy violin, hold breath- less a large crowd of raw recruits, stern old soldiers, and hardy half-wild peasants,

N 2

and fishermen. One and all were melted
into tears, brimmed over with laughter,
or seemed to burn with rage and defiance, as the strain was at first sad,
then wandered into strange crotchets
and quavers irresistibly comic, and ended
in a chorus like that we have just heard."

"We are not quite the stoneyhearted
people you imagine, Signor Mola," said
Lady Lucy Ellerton, "Mr. Beaumont
has infected you with his own disdain
of the English. Remember the enthusiasm our 'God Save the Queen' always
rouses; and that our ballads, 'Auld
Robin Gray,' and the 'Last Rose of Summer,' are the most touching in the world."

"'God Save the Queen' happens, I
believe, to be a German air," put in
Mr. Beaumont; "but even if it was
not, you cannot fairly say that it creates

half the excitement produced by the 'Roast Beef of Old England,' at a public dinner. As to Scotch musical taste, its delicacy is proved by the love of the bag-pipe. A people must have a very sensitive ear, certainly, who can enjoy as they do, the wonderful farrago of sound which ensues when four lusty pipers blare out The 'Campbells are coming.' I once spent a week in a place in the Highlands, where the host was a genuine chieftain, and kept up what he was pleased to call, 'The fine old custom of piping,' at all sorts of un-expected intervals, from dawn to sunset."

"Been in the Highlands, have you, Beaumont," said Bertie Cunninghame, coming up, "then you will know the proper demeanour, and will act Fergus Mc Ivor to perfection, in our Walter

Scott tableaux next week. Would not Beaumont look 'becoming' in a kilt, Fanny, he has just the figure for it?"

"Yes, and I could take him to Matfield Fair next day, and show him at a penny a-head as the Scottish Giant," replied 'Fanny' Ellerton, "with little Tim, my new groom, as the Yorkshire Pigmy, to keep him company."

Beaumont, who was an unwieldy loose made man, of great size, but singular awkwardness, having an immense notion of the grandeur of his own proportions, and of himself in every way, had been slightly flattered by the Mc Ivor suggestion, but was much scandalized at the mere idea of making his appearance in company with a groom at a country fair. He pretended to be occupied in taking a tea-cup from Lady Margaret

Charteris, but as he walked away to put it down, he muttered something which was decidedly the reverse of complimentary to Fanny Ellerton's wisdom.

When not long after this Lady Ferndale and the ladies went to bed, most of the gentlemen adjourned to a large but cosy room, not far from the entrance-door, and opening through a conservatory to the garden. There was a billiard-table at one end, and a comfortable divan and some inviting armchairs round a second fireplace at the other.

The Healey smoking-room had thus the charm of allowing you to play at billiards, without the banishment so often necessary, and yet was big enough for the noise of the balls not to disturb any other men who might

want to talk or read at the opposite
end.

"I had an odd encounter after I
left you the other night, Mola," said
Tresidder, narrating his adventure in
Cavendish Square, "and what made it
more odd, was that the next morning when I called to inquire for the
poor fellow, the daughter merely opened
the door a few inches, and in a sharp
tone informed me that he was much
better, but that I could not enter. This
of course meant that they would not give
me the trouble of coming again, and was
not a very polite way of saying so. I was
sorry, as I had no intention of intruding
upon them, and the daughter's face had
interested me, and hardly now seemed
to agree with the rudeness of her
words. However, of course, I could

only take the plain hint I had received and rid them of my company
at once and for good."

"I am sorry that your good nature in
accompanying me should have brought
you among such churlish associates; but
you are at least consoled by your own
proverb, that virtue is her own re-
ward. What sort of man," continued
Mola, "is our host's son this Lord
Ellerton to whom that peerless Lady
Margaret Charteris is engaged. They
tell me that you have nursed him
through a long illness, indeed have
pulled him out of one that would have
probably been fatal had he received less
kind care."

"Oh! Ellerton would have got well
right enough," replied Michael, "without my appearance on the scene. He

is a fine fellow in many ways, though I suspect, when in strong health, he has a good deal of his mother's pride about him. Once or twice this evening I noticed an expréssion, which seemed the natural interpretation of slight hints I have marked in George's face. He has something, too, of the winning looks which give such a charm to his young brother, Master Fanny, at billiards over there, who seems to be astonishing Bertie's not very weak mind by his wonderful knack in making screws."

"Yes, yes," said Giuseppe Mola, "I daresay Lord Ellerton is good enough to look at, and pleasant enough to make you like him on a sick bed. There are few men whom the act of nursing does not make you fond of.

But is he worthy of that beautiful woman, whose mind is as perfect as her
body."

" You deal in superlative expressions
Giuseppe, but upon my honour I have
known the lady but one evening, and
already think you judge her rightly.
Ellerton is fully sensible of his own
good fortune; when we became intimate, he was continually alluding to
his cousin, and all his schemes of life
seemed to include her. But if it is fair
to speak of this, even in confidence;
during the severity of his illness, when
for a time he talked wildly, it was
his mother's name he uttered most;
and he would often ramble on about
the things she would be proud of his
doing, the prominent part in the world
she wished him to play, and so on.

There seemed to be a bond between
George and Lady Ferndale, natural
enough perhaps between an ambitious
mother and an aspiring proud son.
But after seeing Lady Margaret, it appears a little strange that she should
have been mentioned by her lover rather
as Lucy Ashton the Bride of Lammer-
moor, if she had been as clever as she
was pretty, might have been spoken of
by her brother Douglas, than as the
absolute centre of a man's hopes and sole
mistress of his heart."

"What are you talking about Lucy
Ashton, Michael?" said Bertie Cunninghame, leaving the billiard table; as
much to his disgust young Ellerton
passed him at forty-five, and finished the
game with a marvellously dashing stroke,
which would have been a miss, if played

with twice the care by any other man.
" We are going to exhibit her with
Edgar, Sir William Bucklaw, and all complete belongings, and Signor Mola means
to make his first appearance on any
boards, and to bring down the house
as the romantic Master of Ravenswood.
By-the-bye, you must send to Portruan
for that suit of inlaid armour, standing
in the outer hall, which they have taught
your inguenous mind to believe was worn
by some valiant Tresidder; for you are
to appear as Wilfrid of Ivanhoe, to
Lady Margaret's Rowena, while I under-
take the villain of the scene as Sir Brian
the Templar."

" Very well, Sir Knight, your behest
shall be obeyed," replied Tresidder,
" but may I be allowed to ask, what
is the deep secret of state policy which,

according to Lady Ferndale's letter, you wish to communicate to me. I know that the weight of the British Empire, or rather of its treasury rests mainly upon your mighty arm; but unless you meditate an operation—that is I believe the correct term now-a-days among the high class burglars—with the Bank balances and wish to conceal the plunder at Portruan, I do not quite see how my assistance can be of any use to you."

While his cousin draws Michael aside to answer this question, we may explain that among the numerous avocations, which Mr. Bertie Cunninghame managed to pursue with indifferent success, was that of an active politician. Not that he had any particular convictions as to the real necessity or danger of this or that

measure. Nor that he even pretended to
the electors of Newlyme, when offering to
devote his talents and accomplishments
to the service of that ancient and
persuadeable borough, that it was his
intention to consume the midnight oil
in the study of abstruse constitutional
questions, or the solution of unpleasant
social problems.

He had told them, as he told all
his friends; that it might be very well
for two or three big men in each
generation to go in for such matters,
and that it was a happy thing for other
fellows of more ordinary calibre that
they should do so—but for his part,
so long as there was a free fight
and no favour, the country was pretty
sure to be, in his opinion, fairly governed.
The only thing a man had to do was

to get into the middle of the fray,
and hit out as hard as he could for
his own side, and that ought to be
the side upon which his family had always fought.

If a youngster was so vain of his own
judgment, as to insist on enlisting in
the faction to which his fathers and
grandfathers had been opposed, the
more fool he: but so long as he stuck
to his colours manfully, Bertie could
endure him; but with the shilly-shally
gentlemen, who called themselves independent members, he had no patience
whatever.

"Why the silly fellows would like to
be each his own prime minister,
when they do not know their own
minds for three weeks at a time. A
pretty state the country would be in,

if we had six hundred and forty of
the same kidney sitting in the House
of Commons? Don't talk to me of con-
science! It's nothing, I say, but obstinacy
or conceit; and all because the youths
like to be continually solicited for their
votes by both sides. Grenville, the opposition whip—and a precious good
sort I can tell you for an opponent—
of course always gets hold of them
when he can, and so do I; but we
none the less ever hesitate quietly to join
in breaking a spoke of any wheel they
may try to turn on their own account."

This sort of spirit enabled Bertie to
give, as government whip, invaluable
assistance to his party in making the
young recruits pull well together.
Most of them were sons of rich men,
or in possession of property of their

own; but they had perhaps more of chivalrous readiness to fight under an old banner, than of any very deep acquaintance with questions of state policy.

To such men, it was a real satisfaction to be told that they could not serve their country better than by following the bent of their own inclinations. And the last shadow of scruple they might feel in entering upon a path of such easy virtue was at once dispelled by the assertion, so convincing if made to a high-spirited boy by the object of his former hero-worship at school or college, that there was actually no other course, which a gentleman could pursue with honour.

The mysterious business of the young Lord of the Treasury, on this occasion,

proved to relate to a probable dis-
solution of Parliament in the coming
Spring. The Ministry meant to intro-
duce early next session a bill, which
they knew would be encountered by
the full force of the opposition; and
in the event of their being defeated in
any important division, they had resolved to exercise their right of appeal-
ing to a general election.

Now Cornwall, at that time, returned
no less than four members for the
county, who were all strong opponents
of the government; but many people
of influence, as well as Bertie Cunninghame, considered that a personally
popular candidate, such as the Squire
of Portruan was likely to prove,
would have little difficulty in gaining
one of the seats. To render his

success more sure, it was very desirable that he should make some effort
to become more generally known, than
after so long an absence it was possible for him to be at present.

There was no coming of age, or
other such special cause for festivity:
and it was not wise to excite suspicion
by a sudden effort; but it would be the
most natural thing possible for the Kil-
fenoras to spend at Portruan their
nephew's first solitary Christmas at
home, and of course some other
people could be invited to meet them;
when balls, hunting-breakfasts, and other
entertainments could follow as a matter
of course.

"By all means," said Michael, when
this scheme had been explained to
him; "let Aunt Kilfenora come, and

bring all Ireland in her train. I shall be delighted to see them, and will write to Mrs. Hervey to-morrow, as she does not like being hurried, and will take a couple of months to get the old house fit to receive company, as she calls it. You'll be there, of course, Bertie, to help the affair off;' and we must try before we leave here to get the Ferndales' promise to be of the party.

" By-the-bye, if Lord Sunderland would come also, I should be highly honoured, and it would have a grand effect for the good cause. Then we must ask the Malcolms, and the Trecarrels, and one or two other Cornish people.

" I don't know exactly how many we can put away, but fancy the old house can accommodate two or three and twenty at a pinch. There is lots of room for bachelors in the east wing, and we can take in a whole regiment of servants; but I am a little uneasy about the ladies and the big-wigs. However, no doubt Mrs. Hervey will rise to the occasion."

Having settled, as far as they could, the winter's campaign, Tresidder and Cunninghame rejoined the group round the fire-place, where Fanny Ellerton was delivering an oration on the true principles of male costume. His own smoking attire was more magnifi-cent than was often seen, but, as he said,

"If half the pretty women in London will send me gorgeous smoking-caps and embroidered slippers, as if I was a High Church curate, I am bound in ordinary politeness to dress up to their presents."

In truth, his dark curls and boyish, innocent smoothness of face, with the softest apology for hair on the upper lip only, coupled with his laughing eyes and graceful chivalrous manner, had caused the newest thing in Guardsmen to be the pet of last season, and to have received more bright glances, and listened to more sweet words from dainty lips than often falls to the lot of one fortunate man.

He was always perfectly ready, as who would not be, to submit to any amount of such treatment; but his merry disposition prevented his having been, as yet, greatly spoiled by the process.

"Fellows are so stupid, and will

mix their garments," said this young gentleman, now with all the gravity of a prime minister. "Now a man who is decent looking and a gentleman, can stand almost any strength of colour, so long as he sticks to one, or only picks it out by slight points of a second. Instead of this, a little chap like Harry Wilbraham, comes down to breakfast in a brown coat, a red tie, and a pair of stockings barred with all the colours of the rainbow. Now you can never accuse me of looking gaudy, though I acknowledge that I like to be decently clothed."

Considering that the young gentleman was at that moment clad from head to foot in jacket and loose trowsers of light-brown velvet, trimmed and apparently lined with the loveliest blue silk, while a cap of the same colour, embroidered and tasseled also with blue, was perched jauntingly upon his head, there was no disputing this last proposition. But the only effect of his eloquence upon Bertie Cunninghame was to make him ejaculate—

" Hang it, Fanny, we all know that you were born to be a man-milliner; but, as I have no present intention of rivalling your accomplishments in that line, I vote we all go to bed, or there will be something crooked in our powder to-morrow morning, when we get to the warm corner of the big covert on Hazeldown."

Soon after this, the smokers separated. As Michael said " Good-night" to his cousin at the door of his bedroom, he remarked, with a smile—

"Remember, Bertie, if I do get into the House, I mean to sit as an Independent Member."

Cunninghame rushed at the speaker, who, however, basely avoided the conflict by slipping into the shelter of his room, and quickly shutting the door in the other's face of intense disgust.

CHAPTER X.

EN days had slipped by at Healey Towers as rapidly as pleasant occupations and agreeable society usually cause them to do, and the morning of the much talked of theatricals had arrived. Not a few pheasants had, in the meantime fallen before the guns of Michael Tresidder, Bertie Cunninghame, and young "Fanny" Ellerton, who were all good shots, while many a lively luncheon had been eaten in the great room of the Belvedere, which crowned the highest hill of Healey Park.

With the bright waters of the great lake in the foreground, the windows of this room would have commanded an extensive view over the richly wooded country, had not the prospect been shut out by the trees near to the eye, on the opposite bank of the lake, which had been allowed to grow up too luxuriantly; as it was, the look out was pretty, but confined.

The young ladies, with some one or other of the elders to act *chaperone*, had frequently walked up under Mr. Beaumont and Signor Mola's escort, to lunch with the sportsmen, and once or twice when they had done so, Michael had been tempted to shirk his afternoon's work, and leave his two friends to complete the bag, while he went down to join the merrier riding party.

Every day that had passed, had seemed to him only to bring out some fresh charm of disposition in Lady Margaret Charteris, while every hour was sure to reveal some new phase of her personal beauty, or to place in a new and more captivating light some grace of expression or of attitude, which he had already noticed.

In fact, the young man had fallen in love with this brilliant girl, but as yet was not aware of his own sentiment. Had he been so, since he regarded the lady as practically the wife of another man, and that man his own intimate friend, Tresidder would have despised himself heartily, and have

quickly left the scene of temptation.

Nobody can prevent many emotions
from springing up unbidden in the
heart, which yet are contrary to the
rest of the character. For some time
they may continue to take root, without the individual being conscious of their
existence, and much less of their dis-
honourable nature; but when he does
discover it he flies, if he be a gentleman and a wise man, from every
influence which can foster their growth.
He plucks them out if he can; but if
not he is, unless he be a coward or a
fool, at least able to prevent their
bearing fruit.

On this particular morning all shooting was given up for the day, and
the whole of the *corps dramatique, i.e.,*

nearly all the people staying in the
house, were assembled in the dining-
room for rehearsal under Bertie's super-
intendance. He himself was, at this
moment, perched on a tall pair of
steps, and giving the final touch to
the gold tassels and crimson drapery
of his proscenium.

" What a pity Cunninghame was not
brought up to the sock and buskin
business, is it not, Lady Margaret?"
said Mr. Beaumont, " with his talent
for building a theatre, as well as for
acting, and the little help in the way of
patronage we might all have given him,
he would have realized long before this
a handsome fortune."

" Right for once, Beaumont," interrupted young Ellerton, "he is cut
out for a manager. Perhaps it's not too

late yet; there is certain to be some
theatre to be sold now. I say, Bertie,"
raising his voice, " we are thinking how
charmingly you would do at this sort
of thing in earnest, and Beaumont is
so captivated by your accomplishments,
that he wishes to buy a theatre and set
you up at his own expense."

As that gentleman had plenty of
money, but was notorious for not
liking to spend more of it than was
absolutely needful, Fanny Ellerton's
conclusion made the rest of the party
smile. In order to avoid one of the usual
squabbles between these two, Lady
Margaret called the young Guardsman
to come and help her arrange the
quantity of ferns and other foliage
plants, which were to be massed along
the front of the stage. The dining-

room was very large and lofty, with
an open timber roof of dark oak, and
in shape it was well suited for its
present purposes, being an oblong of
about fifty feet by thirty, with great
bay windows on two sides, a high
carved chimney-piece on the third, and
a large sideboard in a deep recess of
the pannelled wall on the fourth, the
two doors were one at either side
of the fireplace.

The stage took up nearly a third
of the room, at the lower or sideboard end, and was raised some three
feet above the floor. One of the doors
was thus conveniently hidden behind
the proscenium, and by it the actors
were enabled to reach their dressing-
rooms unobserved, as a secondary staircase happened to be just outside.

Through the other, which communi-
cated with one of the drawing-rooms,
the audience would enter to their seats,
which were arranged in tiers one
above the other, while the musicians
were, during the performance, to occupy the recess of one of the bay
windows, also hidden by the proscenium.

Michael's part in the rehearsal was
soon over, and he was sitting with
Miss Clifford on a couch in front of
the stage, when Lord Sunderland entered
with the " Times " of that same morning,
which had just arrived by the day
mail.

" Have you seen this, Mr. Tresidder?" he said, pointing to the first
announcements among the deaths. " What
does it mean? I did not know you

had any relation of your own name, certainly none who could answer such a description."

"Nor have I," answered the young man; "but let me see, what has made you ask?" As he read the lines, however, he looked much puzzled, and then laughing, said, "Oh! this must be some joke of Fanny Ellerton's, what made you give me a relative with such an outlandish christian name, youngster, surely one scriptural denomination is enough for the family."

Then he read aloud—

"October 2nd, at his house in London, Nicholas Tresidder, Esq., of Portruan Manor, Cornwall, aged sixty."

Robert Ellerton listened with such unmistakeably genuine surprise to this paragraph, and the speech which had preceded it, that his denial of any authorship in the transaction was scarcely necessary. While all the rest of the party stopped their rehearsing, and came up in astonishment to examine the paper for themselves; a footman came into the room, with a salver in his hand, and approaching Michael, handed to him the telegraphic letter which was lying upon it.

Tresidder opened the envelope in some haste, and as he read the message, his face changed colour slightly, but only for an instant. Folding the sheet up again, he said, with a smile, which appeared, however, to be somewhat forced—

" This explains the matter, and it is a joke, as I thought; but I beg your pardon, Fanny, for accusing you of perpetrating it."

Then he turned the subject, by asking Lord Sunderland as to the news which the "Times" might contain; and if there were any further particulars of the great explosion of gunpowder which had occurred at Erith a few days before. All the others, of course, followed his lead, and in a few minutes those who had been rehearsing returned to the stage, and the incident was apparently forgotten; though every one, at heart, felt pretty much what young Ellerton expressed in in an under tone to Bertie Cunninghame.

"There is something queer, I am afraid. By Jove, I hope it is not serious! Michael is far too good a fellow to deserve any real bother."

Before very long, Tresidder, who had sat down again by Miss Clifford, and continued to talk for a little while, as if the whole interruption had not occurred, left the room carelessly, and looking about for Lord Sunderland, succeeded in finding him alone in the library writing letters—

" Forgive my interrupting you for a few moments," he said, addressing the statesman, " but if you would not mind the trouble, I should be very glad to show you this telegram, and, perhaps, by-and-by, ask you to advise me, if anything comes of it; you know I have no near relation whom I have a right to consult."

Lord Sunderland at once put aside his letters, and answered in a tone of warm kindness :

"I am very glad you have spoken, Mr. Tresidder, it will always give me the greatest pleasure to be of use to your mother's son, if it is possible; but I hope this business is not really more than a joke."

He looked somewhat grave, however, on reading the following message:

Herbert Townsend, London,
to
Michael Tresidder, Earl of Ferndale's,
Healey Towers,
Matfield.

"Strange announcement in the 'Times' to-day; probably an imposition, but should like to see you soon––to-morrow, if possible; would come to you, if necessary."

Michael said anxiously, as Lord Sunderland finished reading :

" You see, Mr. Townsend, who is my lawyer and a very old friend, does not believe the announcement; but evidently, he thinks it is not quite impossible that it should be true. I know so little myself about my own family, except that I fancy my father came to the property after a distant cousin, that I can form no opinion about it whatever."

" I know Mr. Townsend very well, too," said the Marquis, "and your interests could not be in better or kinder hands. He would have told you if the matter had been really dangerous; but, of course, it will be as well to go up and see him."

"Yes, I will write a line at once to say that I will call about half-past five to-morrow afternoon. I had settled to leave here before, but meant to have paid another visit on the way up to London, if it had not been for this."

"I think that will be best, and hope you will let me know what he says. Remember, I shall never be too busy to hear about your affairs. But," continued Lord Sunderland cheerily, as he sat down again to his own letters, "I do not think you need let this circumstance trouble you, for the present at all events. If this defunct gentleman was really a Tresidder, he is not so now; and even if he was alive, and could claim Portruan itself, he could not touch any of the money your own father made by his mines, nor the land he bought. From what I have heard,

I should suppose the old house and estate produced but a small portion of your income."

Michael Tresidder wrote his note to Mr. Townsend, and then wisely determined to forget, as well as he could, all about this singular interruption to his smooth life. So much so, that during the evening he managed to perform his part in the performance to the satisfaction even of his cousin Bertie.

By a great deal the most successful of the tableaux, was that which presented a fancy representation of Luna. When the curtain drew back, it disclosed a large circle or disc in a screen, which was stretched across the whole front of the stage; while within this moon the figure of the goddess herself appeared, against a background of deep purple velvet.

Her golden hair floated loose over her shoulder, and a large diamond star glittered above her forehead. One white hand and arm was raised, and a taper finger pressed lightly against the ripe curling lips, which were slightly parted; the other arm was allowed to droop, and seemed to be scattering the poppies of which a bunch was in the hand. The robe of the softest white cashmere was made in the Greek fashion, slightly bordered with gold, and powdered here and there with golden stars. Lady Margaret, for it was she, seemed to be rising from clouds of white gauze which were arranged with great art in all the lower part of the picture; while with the same skill, light of extraordinary power had been thrown upon her from behind the screen, so that the whole figure, but especially the face, was brought into the most brilliant relief.

Michael Tresidder, as with the rest of the audience he applauded the charming effect of the tableau, felt that something of the mere prettiness might be due to the young artist who had designed and posed the scene—but that it was the exquisitely pure and delicate face, with its wounderful ex-pression, no less tender than bright, which made the spectator long to fall down and worship a real goddess.

"I have just received a long letter from George," said Lady Ferndale as they were all at breakfast. next morn-ing, "and you will be glad to hear,

Mr. Tresidder, that there really is a
chance of your getting possession of
your own yacht again. My son hopes
to arrange about his selling out in
time to start about the beginning of
December, and means to come home
in the 'Ariel.'"

"Not the pleasantest time of the
year for yachting, I am afraid, Lady
Ferndale, but that is Ellerton's affair.
Does he speak of himself as pretty
strong again?"

"Only by implication, that is he
says nothing at all about his health,
and," with a smile, "I have always
found you gentlemen ready enough to pity
yourselves if there is the least excuse
for it."

Michael Tresidder was to start
very soon after breakfast, but could

not resist the pleasure of exchanging a few last words with Lady Margaret, who had risen from the table, and was standing at one of the open windows, looking out at a herd of does, who were quietly grazing close outside. She had brought some bread with her, and was feeding one of the animals, who was tame enough to eat from her hand. As she did this, there was a pensive, almost sad look upon her sweet face, as different from the brilliant air of the goddess of last night, as was her close fitting morning dress of quiet quaker brown, from Luna's gold embroidered robe.

"You need not be afraid for George, Lady Margaret," said Tresidder, fancying that she might be nervous about the winter voyage. "The 'Ariel' is a

good sea-boat, and December after all
is a better time for sailing than
either Autumn or Spring." As he spoke,
she looked up with the little nod of
playful gratitude, which was one of
her peculiarities and not the least
charming of them; but there was a
wistful look still in her blue eyes.
" Lady Ferndale has promised to come
and pay me a visit in Cornwall next
winter," continued Michael, " and it will
be a great happiness to me, if you
will also honour my house by your
presence. We might write to Ellerton
to run on to Falmouth and join us all.

" My aunt, Lady Kilfenora, whom you
have met in town, is to be there also
with her daughters, who are really
nice girls. Do come, Lady Margaret,
if it will not bore you. I wish so

much to show you our glorious cliffs, and the old house at Portruan has some interesting parts about it."

"Oh! thank you, Mr. Tresidder, for your special invitation; but I had fully meant to come with the rest—unless, indeed, you were unable to receive me," added Lady Margaret, with an arch glance at him. "I have heard much about the beauties of Portruan, and particularly want to make acquaintance with Cornish people and Cornish rocks. They — the people, I mean, not the rocks — are a romantic, emotional race, are they not? and more like Irish peasants than our sober English villagers."

"Yes, perhaps they are in some things; but their tendency is, I think, to be moved to tears rather than to

merriment, like the laughing inhabitants
of the Emerald Isle. Perhaps, however, it is the difference of their
religion. Both are fanatics ; but the
fanaticism of Roman Catholics is a
very different thing from that of Bible-
Methodists, which our people mostly
are. Good-bye, then, Lady Margaret,
for the present. I am proud to think
you are ready to trust yourself to my
charge."

" Good-bye, Mr. Tresidder ; I shall
look forward to Christmas."

As she spoke, Lady Margaret shook
him warmly by the hand, and oddly
enough, the touch of her small fingers
seemed to linger on his through
many a mile of his rapid journey to
town.

On arriving in London, Michael went

straight to Mr. Townsend's office, sending his servant and luggage on to the old quarters in Dover Street. He found that eminent lawyer waiting for him with a large tin box, labelled " Portruan Estate," open by his side, and a deed, which had apparently just been taken from the box, spread out on the table before him.

" I am sorry to bring you up to London; but it was more satisfactory to explain the exact nature of the ground to you at once," said the old gentleman, with his clear decided voice, which harmonised well with the shrewd yet kindly expression of countenance ; " for I daresay you have no conception what this forgery, or, at least, attempt at imposture, has originated in."

He then explained to Michael those limitations of the will, which we have already mentioned, and told him the steps which had been taken by his firm before the Colonel had entered into possession, so as to ascertain, whether or no, Nicholas Tresidder was then still in existence.

" We advertised in three of the morning papers almost every day for nearly two years, and a pretty penny it cost; but your father was determined, rightly enough, to run no risk which he could avoid. We sent men all over the country to make inquiry; we even advertised in New York and Boston, and two or three of the Australian towns; but not a syllable could we hear of this Nicholas, nor of any man at all answering his description. At length your father consented to assume the position of ' Squire.' "

" And from that day," asked Michael, " some twenty-two years since, has there ever been a word of objection to his title, to make you suspect, in the smallest degree, the existence of this man ?"

" Not a shadow nor a syllable," answered the other. "I thought, and my partner, Mr. Farquhar, thought, as we think still, that he would have come forward soon enough, had he been alive. People are not usually backward in claiming a nice estate. We believe this to be the first move in a plot by some impostors, who have learnt the provisions of the will, and who probably think to get money out of you, to silence a claim it may be difficult to disprove."

" They will be disappointed in that," said Tresidder, " at all events. If they can prove their case, I shall give up the place readily enough, though I do not pretend that it would not be a terrible sorrow to me. I would even wish to assist in discovering the real truth, whether it turn out against myself or not. But I will not pay a sixpence to hush the matter up. I may become poor, but I will at least remain honest and a gentleman."

" Yes, yes ; no doubt you are right," replied Mr. Townsend ; " though I should not probably have advised you to take that view of your duty. But as to being a poor man, should the worst come, you do not know what it means. I thought at first, that the only claim any one upon this earth, except yourself, could make to any of your possessions, is to the original Portruan property, which amounts to some three thousand a-year at the outside."

"So Lord Sunderland said," answered Tresidder; "but I fear that I should think that a poor consolation if they could touch the old house itself, every room and every part of which is associated with my dear mother, and our happy life together."

"Yes, yes; but these scoundrels will claim all the additional land your father bought, more than twice as much as what he inherited, as part of the entailed estate; since it was bought with the fines of the mineral leases.

"Well, well, my friend, I do not wonder that this sounds bad to you, but remember they have not got any yet. If they had a particle of evidence, they would have begun the attack, you may be sure, in some more formal manner than this. I thought it was better that you should know at once exactly how the land lies. But I tell you fairly, that, in my opinion, if, as we intend, you take no notice whatever of this, and if you go down to Cornwall, as you had meant to do, and live openly and actively at Portruan, they will see that we are not afraid of them, nor even think them worth a thought; and ten to one we never hear a word more about this Nicholas **Tresidder** or anyone connected with him."

Then turning to another subject, Mr. Townsend said,

"Now I wish to ask you, as to this piece of land the New Railway wish to buy; I have the conveyance ready for your signature."

The lawyer touched his hand-bell, and asked for the deed.

"Mr. Turnwell had it to engross, Sir," said the clerk; "but no doubt it is finished by this time. I will send him."

After a few minutes, during which the former topic of their conversation was not again mentioned, Philip Turnwell entered the room with a large sheet of parchment in his hand, covered with the large round handwriting of a legal document, and headed with some words in that quaint old English orthography, which profane outsiders have begun to think is emblematic of the antiquated and absurd intricacy which still encumbers much of our system of law.

Mr. Townsend got up from his own chair, and standing by that of Tresidder, was pointing to the place for him to sign, when he chanced suddenly to look up at Philip, who was on Michael's other side. The old lawyer was for a moment startled, to the point of losing his self-control, by the wonderfully intent and eager look with which his clerk was peering down into the tin deed box, which was still open on the floor, and by the expression of bitter malice, and yet triumph, which the young man's features bore. He recovered himself, however, in another instant, and moving carelessly back to his chair, managed by the merest accident, as it appeared, to close the lid of the deed box, by stumbling against it as he passed.

Nothing was said, and not until Michael and Philip had both left the room some time, did Mr. Townsend think more of what he had witnessed. Then, as he was preparing to leave his chambers for the day, he suddenly exclaimed, half aloud—

"Confusion! I really believe that fellow Turnwell is at the bottom of the plot. At all events, I will take extremely good care that he does not get any possible chance of hatching his abominable schemes in my office."

Sending for one of his superior clerks, he said—

"By-the-by, has not that man, Philip Turnwell, been extremely irregular in his attendance for some months? I

remember you complained of it last
year, too. We do not want dissipated
fellows here, and you may as well in-
form him that his services can be
dispensed with after this week. He
will be entitled to a month's salary, of
course."

CHAPTER XI

RUTH TURNWELL had been true to her word. She had persisted in the refusal to allow her brother to have anything to do with the old man's burial, and had scraped together, by the sale of nearly all the articles of scanty furniture their room had contained, the few pounds necessary for that purpose, and for her own mourning.

Philip had been willing to contribute,

not from any awakening of filial affection, but because of the interest
with which he now regarded his father,
as being the link which united himself
to possible riches. He had sent the
announcement, which we have seen, to
the " Times," and although, until the evidence of his claim was more complete,
he did not purpose to attract attention
to himself by assuming the name of
Tresidder, he had wished his sister to
do so, and had even offered to make
her some small weekly allowance. In
fact, he knew her to be an important
witness as to the finding of the papers,
and feared that she would embarrass
him seriously by carrying out her
present intention of leaving London,
and concealing her future place of
abode.

Once more they were together in the Compton Street lodging, a poor place enough when we first visited it, but utterly miserable and desolate now, with literally nothing on the bare floor beyond the pallet-bed in the corner, and piled together in the middle the old violin-case and a couple of boxes, containing the few clothes Ruth possessed. On one of these boxes she was sitting, the deep black of her dress sharpening the outline of her features, but at the same time heightening their pathos, since the sombre colour harmonised well with the expression of weary grief, which, since her great sorrow, had become habitual to her face.

"Not many women," said Philip, who had been trying in vain to shake his sister's resolution to keep her life sepa-

rate from his, " would be so short-
sighted as to leave a brother, who was
on the point of becoming rich. The
certificate of our father's marriage is
the only important piece of evidence
that I now require, and Burrows is
pretty sure to rout that out before
long. Of course, when I have got the
estate, I shall make a suitable provi-
sion for you."

" Possibly you might," replied Ruth,
" some feeling of family pride might then
cause you to remember the natural ties
of blood, which, up to this time, you
have managed to forget altogether. If
you became owner of Portruan Manor,
you might be ashamed to have it known
that your sister was working for her
bread. But you have no reason to fear,
for I am more ashamed of the rela-

tionship than you can ever be, and will see that there shall be nothing to connect us in the eyes of the world."

"You will act with your usual amiability, no doubt," sneered Philip, "and the more so that you know your evidence to be a principal part of my case."

Then, changing his tone,

" I cannot see why you should hate me more decidedly than ever, as it seems, since this chance has appeared. I could not bring poor father to life again if I would; and in endeavouring to obtain this fortune, I am only trying to get what is, in fact, my own. You could not be more bitter, if I was plotting some robbery."

" Perhaps you are right, Philip, and

I am bitter; but you find it easy to forget all the past, and to think only of this prospect of riches before you. I cannot do that in this room, especially. I must think more of all the misery you have brought, during the last few years, upon him who is gone. But for you, he would never have sunk so low as this; but for you, he might be alive now, for quiet and happiness are powerful medicines. He struggled on bravely, and in spite of your frequent applications, and of his own misfortunes, he had still managed to keep a decent place in the world, and even to preserve a small sum at the bank; when your wretched forgery swept all away.

"To save you from punishment he had,

in addition, to sell all but the very bed
on which he has died, and the table
and few chairs, which have now gone,
to pay for his burial. After you had
utterly ruined him, he was, I suppose,
of no further use to you, and that is
why you have kept aloof. Had he
been a stranger in blood, you might
have spared something for his comfort out of the good salary he sa-
crificed so much to prevent your
losing."

"Well, well, I have said that I am
sorry, there is no use in continually
raking up byegones. He might have
been rich enough, if he had chosen.
Why should he spoil all my life, and
yours, because he chose to be obsti-
nate, as well as his own. Half the
wrong things in the world would not

be done, if the temptation to them was
not so great. I will not say that because he chose to live himself, and bring
me up in a false position, he is properly the cause of every little thing
that I may have done wrong; but I
do consider, and even you, Ruth, must
acknowledge, that I have never had fair
play."

"You call forgery a little thing, do
you? and complain that a father who
half starved himself 'for your pleasures
did not give you 'fair play?' But I cannot wrangle now, I am too sick at heart.
Let us settle once for all this question
between us. I love the name which
he chose to bear, for his sake; and
I do not care for the grand estate
which could never remind me of my

father. I intend to remain still Ruth Turnwell, and to keep myself, as I have said, separate, always separate from you. But I wish to act fairly. On this condition only, that you do not attempt to trace me, or thrust yourself upon me; I will promise to come forward at the right time and give the evidence you require. When is the trial to be, and where? In London I suppose?"

"No, in Cornwall, at Bodmin: and probably in the Spring. February, or March, next year. You must have your own way, of course, but how am I to communicate with you?"

"Oh! that is easy enough, when next February comes, I will watch for some paragraph in the 'Times,' and will come to the appointed place.

Now," said the girl, rising without any attempt to conceal her pleasure at the termination of their interview, " I wish you till then good-bye, God knows that I shall be glad enough if you should prove that my estimate of your character is a false one."

Philip had no resource, but to be content with the amount of promised assistance which he had obtained, and to acquiesce now in his sister's plainly intimated wish that he should leave her.

In truth, he had not expected to gain so much even as this from her, and as he walked from the room he shook the coldly-offered hand warmly, ignoring in his gratitude the stern comments upon his character, with which she had accompanied the concession. It makes no difference to a cur, so long as he gets his bone, whether it is bestowed caressingly, or thrown with a kick or a curse at his head.

Little as her brother's society brought of comfort, Ruth scarcely realised in full her utter solitude in the world until after his departure. This had been the day of Nicholas Turnwell's funeral, and up to this time, strange and sad as it may appear, she had derived companionship from the presence in their room of the coffin which held all that remained of him upon the earth. Now even that vestige of sympathy was gone, and except for the man, whom she had just sent away, and of whom the mere sight stirred her anger, she was alone, absolutely alone.

She was not, however, by her disposition, naturally inclined to sit with her hands before her, weakly repining at the inevitable. The struggle, which had already been her lot in life, had taught her, comparatively young as she was, the lesson that some statesmen even are not wise enough in late maturity to apprehend. She accepted as conclusive the "logic of accomplished facts," and had already decided upon her own course, and made some arrangement for the future. Her knowledge of music was, as we have said, considerable, and by great industry during all her spare hours, she had also acquired a more than usually accurate acquaintance with modern litera-

ture and history, and had made herself a fair linguist.

Having at once determined to leave
London, Ruth had asked the great
musician at whose performances she
assisted, to recommend her as a gover-
ness anywhere in the country, and
through him had fortunately been already successful in obtaining an en-
gagement, and was to start for the
distant scene of her new life this
evening.

It seemed to her a singular coinci-
dence, that this should be in the very
county where she had now, in all
probability, a right to a very different
position; but she could not guess that
her new pupil was daughter of the
vicar of the very parish in which her
mother had resided, and in whose

church her hurried wedding with Nicholas
Turnwell had taken place thirty years
ago.

Cornwall, unlike the rest of the
kingdom, has been apparently retiring
further and further from London, as
the means of locomotion have become
more rapid. When it occupied several
days to reach Exeter, and only one
more to get on to Truro or Falmouth,
people did not consider the difference
between the end to be relatively
great.

Devonshire was out of the world,
and its sister county only a little more
so. But the result of some five and
twenty years of railway progression has,
so far as the West of England is concerned, been almost comical. You can
now reach the capital of one country

in about five hours, but you cannot arrive at the chief town of the other in much less than eleven; *i.e.,* in about the same time as it would take you to travel to Paris, Dublin, or Edinburgh.

Ruth, however, who had all her life been confined to London and its immediate neighbourhood, was too glad to leave behind, as far as possible, the place associated with her severe struggles in the past, and of her present great sorrow, to dislike the long night journey necessary to reach Bodmin, or even the twenty miles of rather dismal drive, which lay between that town and Penaluna Vicarage.

She had, moreover, learnt by hard necessity to make her own way in life, and as the mail-train rushed on through the

darkness, she felt little of that nervous
dread of a new home, which would
have tormented many a girl of her
age, whose course hitherto might have
been through bright sunshine, and under
the shelter of kind friends. The sterner
part of her disposition, with which she
confronted the outside world, experienced a slight sensation of curiosity
as to the future, and that was all;
while the wealth of loving tenderness
which lay deep down in her heart, was
exclusively lavished upon the remem-
brance of her dead father.

Indeed, as it turned out, the
small family circle of which she was
to form part, was not very formid-
able ; and when at length she did
arrive at the end of her journey, the
genuine kindness with which she was

at once made welcome, caused her to experience a new sensation, and to understand by experience, for the first time, something of what may be conveyed by the expression—quiet domestic happiness.

END OF THE FIRST VOLUME.

LONDON :

Printed by A. Schulze, 13, Poland Street.